O9-BUD-812

3 7557 00029 7891

9-14

WITHDRAWN

Moweaqua Public Library
600 N. Putnam
Moweaqua, IL 62550

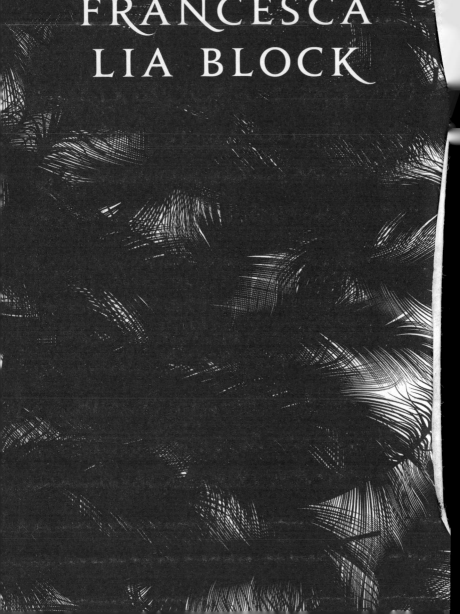

FRANCESCA
LIA BLOCK

PRAISE FOR

LOVE IN THE TIME OF GLOBAL WARMING

A Top Ten Title on the 2014 Rainbow List

A Junior Library Guild selection

"[B]eautifully written . . . Penelope is no buff, bold hero but a grieving, relatable girl 'stuffed full of fear.'" —*The Washington Post*

★ "A post-apocalyptic setting awash with danger brings an exhilarating twist to Block's signature mashup of rock-and-roll urchins and high literature. . . . Literary-minded readers will enjoy teasing out the allusions to Homer . . . but knowledge of the classics is not a requirement to be swept up in the tatterdemalion beauty of the story's lavish, looping language."

—*Publishers Weekly*, **starred review**

"The juxtapositions, too, are pulled off flawlessly: the disgusting, deathly, anxious, and devastating are, improbably—through Pen's astute eyes—also beautiful, lively, serene, and hopeful. Block achieves these and other heroic literary feats in this sophisticated melding of post-apocalyptic setting, re-imagined classic, and her signature magical realism."   —*The Horn Book*

"Magic is no stranger to Block's world, nor is her signature poetic sensibility. And love, in its many varieties and forms, is celebrated, as always."   —*Booklist*

"The dreamlike quality of the writing, typical of the author's works, functions well with the fantastical elements of the story. . . . This is an excellent title for students who have read Homer's *Odyssey* as well as readers who enjoy a mix of fantasy and reality."

—*School Library Journal*

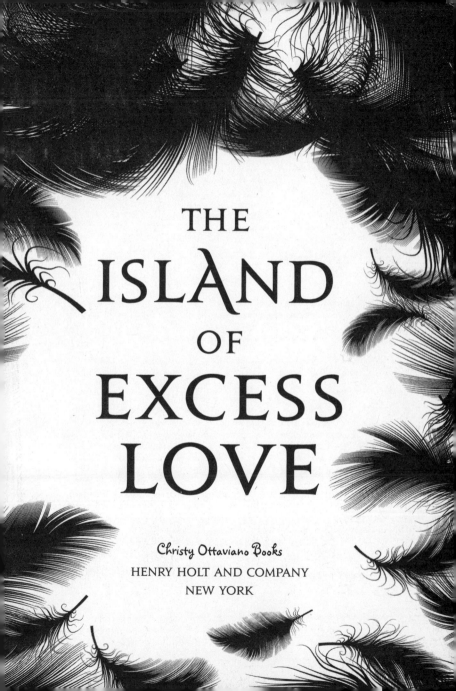

THE
ISLAND
OF
EXCESS
LOVE

Christy Ottaviano Books

HENRY HOLT AND COMPANY
NEW YORK

I would like to thank Laurie Liss, Christy Ottaviano, Jeffrey Hirsch,
Amy Allen, Allison Verost, April Ward, Neil Swaab, George Wen,
Lara Stelmaszyk, Jasmine, and Sam.

Henry Holt and Company, LLC
Publishers since 1866
175 Fifth Avenue
New York, New York 10010
macteenbooks.com

Henry Holt® is a registered trademark of Henry Holt and Company, LLC.
Copyright © 2014 by Francesca Lia Block
All rights reserved.

Henry Holt books may be purchased for business or promotional use.
For information on bulk purchases, please contact Macmillan Corporate
and Premium Sales Department at (800) 221-7945 x5442 or
by e-mail at specialmarkets@macmillan.com.

Library of Congress Cataloging-in-Publication Data
Block, Francesca Lia.
The island of excess love / Francesca Lia Block.
pages   cm
Companion to: Love in the Time of Global Warming.
Summary: Pen, Hex, Ash, Ez, and Venice are living on hard work, companionship,
and dreams in the pink house by the sea until a foreboding ship arrives and all start
having strange visions of destruction and violence then, trancelike, they head for the
ship and their new battles, with Pen using Virgil's epic *Aeneid* as her guide.
ISBN 978-0-8050-9631-6 (hardback)—ISBN 978-1-62779-239-4 (e-book)
[1. Survival—Fiction.   2. Friendship—Fiction.   3. Love—Fiction.   4. Visions—
Fiction.   5. Virgil. Aeneid.   6. Los Angeles (Calif.)—Fiction.   7. Science
fiction.]   I. Title.
PZ7.B61945Isl 2014   [Fic]—dc23   2014005284

First Edition—2014 / Designed by April Ward

Printed in the United States of America

1   3   5   7   9   10   8   6   4   2

For Christy

One day—who knows?—even these
will be grand things to look back on.

From Virgil's *The Aeneid*

THE VERY YOUNG ALCHEMIST *stared at the people flying off the buildings on the TV screen. For one heart-banging beat he wondered if they had discovered the magic spell to make them fly.*

It was not that.

The plane had crashed through the buildings.

His mother came in, turned off the TV, and told him to go to his room and get ready for school.

Instead he went to his sister's room; she was seated on the floor, her three black hound dogs sitting upright behind her, her black, red, and yellow-striped snake asleep in its cage. Black candles burned and a sketchbook lay open. There was an image on the page of a naked man and woman holding each other in a fountain. The man wore antlers on his head and the woman was missing one eye. Next to it was another image—two skeletons in the same intertwined position with roses growing on and among their bones. A third image was of a young boy with a white dove, both surrounded by symbols.

His sister looked up at him pale-bluely, her eyes so like his that it sometimes confused him.

"Did you see the TV?" he said.

"I felt sick all night," she answered.

He didn't know what this meant. That she'd seen it? That she hadn't because she was sick? That she was sick because she knew what happened before it happened? The last option was not unlikely if you happened to be his sister.

"Can I stay here?" he asked.

She shrugged and he sat down on the floor with her. The curtains were drawn and the room was dim although it was morning. Her hair seemed to be the only source of light.

"This world sucks," he said.

His sister ignored him

"What are you doing?"

She looked up and stared at him again with her faintly shining eyes. "Witchcraft. Magic. What do you think I'm doing?"

"I want to learn."

"You don't learn it. You either have the gift or not."

"What are you going to do?"

The three dogs, who had remained almost motionless, began to bay, as if at the full moon of her presence. "I'm going to change the world," she said.

She never did. Not even in the little ways that everyone does, except by changing his world when she left it. The gift? He achieved it. But by then it was too late.

1

CONFLAGRATION

Now that I can no longer believe in God or gods or goddesses, I pray each night to my dead mother, Grace, that we will survive another day and be able to stay here in the pink house on the edge of the world, that my friends and my brother and I will be safe, the plants in our garden will continue to grow, and the water in our spring will not dry up. As far as the rest of the planet after the Earth Shaker? I don't even know where to begin. . . .

My parents weren't religious, but before each meal when Venice and I were little we would hold hands and say, "Thank you for the food, god and goddess," our own tiny prayer. I guess all the myths my parents read us were a kind of religion. The myths and the images in the art books my mother collected. But there aren't many books or paintings left now. My friends and I intend to make as many of our own as possible.

Ezra—or Ez, as we call him—is our resident painter. Today he is painting another portrait of Ash who poses draped in a sheet, his feet bare and firmly planted, his dreadlocks tied back, his eyes darkly seductive. The final painting, inspired by the symbolist painter Franz von Stuck, will depict Ash as an angel winged and playing a horn; I've seen the sketches. It's appropriate to paint Ash with those broad gold wings because he told us that when the Earth Shaker hit, the wind blew him across the desert and landed him inside the body of the T-Rex statue in Cabazon where we found him. The horn in the painting will symbolize Ash's musical powers; he once charmed a monster into submission with it.

Ez has superpowers of his own; during the Earth Shaker he was able to save himself from being crushed by a toppling bookcase.

And there's the power of his art, which, in its realism and magic, seems almost as mysterious.

Ez took the wings from his imagination and memory but at least he has a real young man to paint, and one he

adores at that. I'm not sure if there are any winged creatures in this world, let alone many other young men. In the
days since Ez and Ash and Hex returned to me from
the dead—or so it seemed—we haven't seen anyone
else. I'm relieved every day that no one has come looking
for us, trying to harm us or steal our food, but relief
turns to a cold hollow in my belly when I think that there
may not be anyone out there to come. There may be
Giants like Kutter, the one who spared my life when
I told him the story of how he was cloned by his maker,
Kronen. Or Kutter's brother, Bull, whom I blinded with
my only weapon at the time—a pair of scissors.

I'm more relieved about the fact that we haven't seen
more Giants than about anything else. There's no way to
explain what it feels like to be engulfed in those fleshy,
greasy palms, to smell a Giant's fetid breath or feel their
blood splash against your skin. No Giants here, though, just
us, as if we're in some sort of protected zone they can't pen-
etrate. Because I think they're out there somewhere. How
else could this many humans and animals have vanished so
quickly? The Earth Shaker didn't kill that many on its own.
I believe there are Giants savaging what's left of the world.

Ash gazes into Ez's eyes as Ez paints him; they
could do this all day. Not that I blame them; I stare at
Hex any chance I get. I just don't paint well enough to

capture him on canvas. So instead I tell myself this running story about him, everything he says and does. Like right now: he's reading a musty copy of *The Aeneid* by Virgil in my father's old armchair, the faint light of afternoon that has broken through the omnipresent clouds coming in the window. My beloved is dressed in his usual black clothes, his so-black-it-looks-blue hair slicked back from his face, showing off his widow's peak and making his eyes look even bigger than they normally do. Hex's skin is so pale and thin you can practically see through it and sometimes I wish I really could: look right at his heart. That heart, it saved my life, just by the fact of it surviving the end of the world and finding me.

"'Excess of love, to what lengths you drive our human hearts!'" Hex reads aloud, as if he knows my thoughts. *The Aeneid* is the story of how the hero Aeneas founded Rome. When Hex discovered the book on my parents' bookshelves he freaked out and made us all read it; he still shares passages with us throughout the day. "As you may recall, that's when Aeneas betrays Queen Dido's love and leaves her to go start a new civilization." Sometimes Hex likes to play schoolteacher.

"'Excess of love,'" I say. "What is that, even? How can there be an excess of love?" I want to go over and kiss his lips. They look as soft as they feel. I imagine his sharp teeth hiding under them.

"If it blinds you to the truth. If it paralyzes you and keeps you from taking action," he says, without looking up from his book. I realize I'm jealous of an ancient Roman poet who died in 19 B.C. He was a man, too, so it shouldn't bother me; Hex is definitely all about the girls. But his remark worries me.

Sometimes, especially after losing my left eye, I wonder if I'm blind to the truth but if so I don't really care, as long as my illusion includes my loved ones.

I go over and sit at Hex's feet, running my hands up the leg of his jeans to feel the warmth on my cool skin, feel the way his calf muscles bunch up. "Come help me make dinner," I say.

"Virgil is my new favorite poet," he says, not really hearing me.

I pout, making my mouth look, I hope, like Ez's muse Ash's full lips always do, even in repose. I thought Hex's favorite poet was Homer, whose *Odyssey* seemed to parallel our lives to an uncanny extent. "Didn't you reread *The Aeneid* again last week?"

"Yes, but now I'm reading it for inspiration." Hex stops and looks up at me from under the arrow of his hairline. "I'm going to write an epic poem." And then he adds, "For you," and grins, making me forget that I was ever annoyed with him. Hex has a way of doing that. Maybe one advantage of being alone on the planet, or at least the continent, is that I don't have to compete with any pretty girls for his attention. I'm his only muse, his only lover, and he's all mine.

"Pen!"

My little brother, Venice, is shouting my name as he tromps in from the garden with our dog, Argos. I hear two boy-feet in worn-out sneakers and four prancing paws on the kitchen linoleum. "The pumpkin's ready!"

If Ez, Ash, Hex, and I are busy with our stories and paintings, my brother has the most important work of all. He's in charge of the food supply and it's like his hands are charmed; he can coax fruits and vegetables from the slushy ground outside our home. If people once considered roses or diamonds the highest compliment, now we all feel that way about a cauliflower or an apple.

Venice's pumpkin is small and round, a glossy orange color. At another time—we call it Then—we would have carved a face and put a candle inside. Children dressed as demons would have come to our door asking for candy. Now we pray every day that real demons don't come and that there will be enough food to last us through the uncertainty ahead.

In the garden, the vines grow over the gazebo Hex

and Venice built and the baby pumpkins hang like small lanterns, but we didn't expect this one to ripen so fast. Of course, Venice's garden isn't like any other so it's not that surprising. When I arrived back at this house after my journey I buried the hallowed bones of Tara, the sacred girl the Giants killed. Ever since, under Venice's care, things seem to grow in our garden as if they are charmed.

If I were a plant, I'd be charmed by Ven: his dove-gray eyes and the way he coos like a dove, too, while he works, the way he tries to hide his smile by shifting his gaze and pressing his lips together.

He's shot up in the last few months and he can outrun me when we venture out to race around the periphery of the house, but he's still my little brother. He's the one I always worried about before there was any real reason to worry and the one I thought I'd lost forever when the danger exceeded anything I could ever have imagined.

Venice, Argos, and I go into the kitchen where my mother used to cook for us. Those great dinners; I took them all for granted until she was gone, swept away by the storm that followed the Earth Shaker and then by the hand of one of Kronen's Giants. The kitchen still reminds me of my mother so much—the blue and white tiles she hand painted with flowers and animals, the big wooden table where she served us breakfast, the window overlooking the garden. Missing her doesn't feel like such a terrible thing anymore. It lets me know that her memory is still within me; she's gone but she's here, too. That's one thing my journey taught me about loss. Or maybe I just have to believe this because otherwise I would have perished from grief by now.

My parents might be gone, the sea has encroached on most of the garden, and there's no functional refrigerator or stove, but I still find the kitchen one of the most comforting parts of the house.

Venice sets the pumpkin on the counter and we admire its even striations and jaunty stem. My stomach is growling already. We might have an enchanted garden but food is still scarce these days. There are no animals to hunt even if we could bear the idea of killing one. The Giants have devoured them all. Every so often we even get secret deliveries of canned and bottled goods, candles and matches, and even clothes and shoes. We never see who leaves them in the night and I've never caught the person, though I've tried. I'm pretty sure it's Merk, whom we consider our strange-angel guardian, otherwise known as my genetic father, the one who saved me from my enemy Kronen and his men three times, although not before Kronen had taken my eye.

I put my hand up to the patch I wear, reflexively,

every time I think of how Kronen bobbed his head at me, pursing his lips, gleefully stroking that little beard; the way it felt to thrust my sword through Kronen's jacket made of dried skin and into him, into a human body, when he tried to have me killed. Killing someone is the last thing I thought I'd ever do. But I never expected my life to be like this.

Here I am, unable to consider killing an animal but I actually killed a man, using just a sword. I used to be a girl who went to high school, stayed home on weekends studying the encyclopedia, art history, and mythology, whose greatest heartbreak was an unrequited crush on my best friend, Moira, and the possibility of losing our home to foreclosure when my father lost his job. Now I'm a one-eyed killer without a father or a mother or a world. My brother and my friends tell me that I'm a hero but I feel like that was all accidental and I hope it's behind me. I've learned to accept my half vision and consider the loss of my eye and my innocence the price I had to pay for being able to return to my home, find Venice, and reunite with Hex, Ez, and Ash.

They come into the kitchen as if my thought conjured them.

"Pumpkin stew?" Ez says, rubbing his hands together. He's our best chef. "I'll roast the seeds for on top and even cook the onions in some olive oil tonight." The oil appeared on the doorstep with the last mysterious delivery.

"There's kale for salad," Venice adds, pulling a dark green head of ruffled leaves from his pocket, and even Hex smiles. My junk-food lover has really changed his ways; he hardly ever mentions cheeseburgers or diet soda anymore. It's as if that life, Then, was a dream we had.

Or maybe this is the dream? As long as I have my boys with me I'll take it; I'll stay asleep.

After dinner and cleanup Hex leads us in our nightly group meditation where we sit in a circle breathing and trying to clear our minds.

Tonight Hex wants us to tell what we're afraid of and when it's my turn I say, "Having to leave here."

"Me, too," Ez echoes.

"Why?" asks Hex. He always wants to get to the root of our feelings.

"Because I don't think I can take any more of the real world," I admit.

"As long as we have each other you can." It's the first thing Venice has contributed to the discussion and makes me smile in spite of myself.

"And you're stronger than you realize, Pen," Ash adds and Ez nods and squeezes my hand.

But I don't feel strong; I feel like a small, fragile

Cyclops. Like a Cyclops, one-eyed, wrecked from battle. This Cyclops would rather go back to sleep than get up, face the world, and fight again. My expression must give that away.

"You're a storyteller," Ez reminds me. "That's heroic."

"How is that heroic?"

"Well, you make up some wicked cool words," Ash teases. "*Schnuzzle? Thrombing?* Come on, that's priceless."

"And potentially life saving," Ez contributes solemnly.

"Very funny."

Venice's gray eyes get that light-filled, dreamy look. "You have to imagine things before you can do them. Stories help us see."

"The story is the seed, the action the flower," Hex says.

"How do you define heroism?" I ask him.

"'And though his heart was sick with anxiety, he wore a confident look and kept his troubles to himself.' Virgil, speaking of the hero Aeneas who must emerge from his defeat in the Trojan War and sacrifice many things in order to found a new civilization."

"'Kept his troubles to himself.'" That pretty much describes Hex. "Which means you can't tell us what you're afraid of?"

"Bad hair?" Ash winks at Hex.

I pull on one of Ash's faunish dreadlocks. "That's you more than him."

"Well first, ow. And second, I don't want to go out there either." He frowns through the window at the encroaching night. "No matter how strong Pen here is."

"You're all forgetting your strength," Hex says, a slight snarl to his upper lip.

"You still didn't answer Pen's question," Ez challenges. "Or maybe you're not afraid of anything?"

Hex sits up straighter and glares at an invisible spot a few inches in front of his face. "'Must you make game . . . with shapes of sheer illusion?'"

Ash flings his hair back over his shoulder. "Say what?"

"It's a passage where Aeneas is talking to his mother, the goddess Venus, who helped the Trojans. She kept rescuing her son when Athena, the goddess on the side of the Greeks, tried to harm him, but Venus always came in disguise. To answer your question, I'm afraid of illusions."

And the words crawl up my vertebrae to the nape of my neck.

Later we all say good night and head to bed. We are trying to conserve our candles for emergencies and so our days are determined by the rising and setting of the sun. I don't mind because I have Hex to sleep with. He's my personal flame.

We hold hands as we walk upstairs to my room, our

fingers woven like threads making a quilt, a quilt that would tell a story of our battles, our separation, and our reunion. Argos always sleeps with his nose tucked into the curve of his body at the foot of Venice's bed in the room next door to mine, and Ez and Ash have my parents' old bedroom.

The floorboards creak under our feet, swollen with moisture that seems to have seeped into the entire house. I shiver with cold and with the anticipation of being held in my lover's arms. When we reach the bed Hex faces me, takes my right hand, and holds it up to his chest so I can feel his heart, yes, *throbbing* under the tattoo that reads *Heartless*. Hex is the most heart-ful person I know but he likes to pretend he's "badass," as he would say. And he is that, too. He's the one who taught me to sword fight, who fixed the leaking roof and scavenged for pieces of unbroken glass to replace the windows that were smashed in the maelstrom. Our pink two-story clapboard house might not be moisture proof but it's pretty safe and solid compared with anything else I've seen out there—well, except for the Giant's lairs but those don't count.

"Feel that?" Hex says. "An excess of love, baby." His pulse is so strong I can imagine the whole shape of his heart, as if I'm holding it in my cupped palm.

I put his hand to my heart, too. "No such thing."

He lifts me up—even though we're about the same height he's always been stronger—and lays me on the bed. I shiver, cold until he eradicates the chill with the length of his warm body, his face buried against my collarbone so his hair tickles my chin. Outside I can hear the sea, our music mix. Sometimes I wonder what's out there in that ocean, if any life is there, if a world still exists on other shores. Were the Earth Shaker, and the tsunami that followed, felt around the planet? Did other Giants decimate the population? I could wonder all night but now I just want to pray to my mother and listen to Hex's heartbeat, just want us to remain in our secret place until we die.

"Why are you afraid of illusions?" I whisper to Hex as I taste the first intoxicating petal of the flower of sleep.

"Because I think we're all going unconscious here in some way. And we can't afford to. We have to be strong. You never know what's coming."

It's almost enough to make me snap awake. But not quite.

I dream about my mother, Grace. She's in my room with me—it's so real. I can see her long hair and her white nightgown blowing in a salt-sea breeze that's come through the window. Her eyes are the same bright gray as Venice's eyes. There's a coronet of gold and baroque pearls on her head and a white dove perched on her hand. She looks young and healthy, not the frail near-corpse I held in my arms just before we were separated for the last time. All this BS about being okay with the loss of her, as long as I have her memory, is gone. My heart is atrophying. Even in my sleep I feel tears dripping hot streaks down my face, taste their salt in my mouth. I reach for her, once, twice, three times, but each time she escapes me.

I know that my mother wants me to leave, go somewhere, but I don't understand. She wants me to go to Paris? Athens? Rome? Venice! My mother loved that city the most, obviously; that's why she named my brother after it. I remember our trip to Europe when I was ten. It didn't seem like a real place to me at the time—the gondolas, the little canals running between the ancient, ornate buildings. Does Venice, Italy, even exist anymore? But that's not what my mother means. No, something else. She wants me to go away from the house, to do something important. She shows me a tiny painting she's made. It's of a man with overlarge, palliative blue eyes, flared nostrils, full lips. And a crown of antlers on his head.

I ask her who he is and she says he's the king and that I must go find him. I ask if she can go with me. It's the only way I can do it, I say. She shakes her head, no, she can't. I'll have to do this by myself. The world is depending on you, she says.

What world?

The next day I wake with Hex spooning me. It's so cozy-dozey here, and warm, why would I ever want to get up? But something propels me. In spite of the cold and the veil of sleep still clinging to my body, I go to the window. The sky is its usual gray, not even a few streaks of rose glimmering through the clouds, and the sea just outside our house is liquefied lead.

On its surface, moored against a rock I see a wooden ship, creaking softly—perhaps that is the sound that woke me. The large tattered sails flap in the wind. A coldness goes through me as if I've been immersed in the morning ocean and goose bumps blast up on my arms and shins.

Before I can wake Hex I hear the front door open and see a figure run out of the house toward the ship in the water. Venice.

"I'm coming!" he cries. He is stumbling and falling, getting up again and running with his arms outstretched.

I race downstairs, through the kitchen, and out the back door.

"Venice! Stop! What is it?"

He doesn't seem to hear me. As I catch up with him and touch his shoulder he turns and stares. I realize he is sleepwalking—that blank expression. Sleepwalking was something that terrified me as a child—lack of consciousness in motion, like the reanimated dead, the revenants who peopled those old black-and-white zombie films played on TV at witching hours. I say his name again.

"There's something out there," Venice whispers, his sea-gray eyes pooling bigger.

And then my little brother's hair bursts into flame.

2

OMENS

STOP. DROP. ROLL.

I throw myself on top of Venice, and I'm screaming, screaming for Hex who knows the ways of fire. I can smell the bitter char of burning hair, hear the sizzle but I don't care if I burn to death; my brother is not going to be harmed. He's the one who has to survive in this post–Earth Shaker world. He's the reason I survived this long. Maybe my sole purpose is to sacrifice myself for him.

All these thoughts rage through my mind like flames as I tackle my brother, trying to put out the fire with my own body and the wet ground.

The next thing I know, Hex is holding me, saying my name over and over and telling me to look. I don't want to look. I don't want to see any more destruction. I can't take this loss, above all.

"I'm all right, Pen, I'm okay." It's his voice—Venice—and I force myself to open my eye.

"What happened?" I reach to touch his hair. It's all there, longer on top, shorter on the sides, neatly trimmed by Ez's scissors just a few days ago, as if Venice had gone to a professional salon. We teased him then. Feels so long ago.

"What happened, Hex? I saw it. . . ."

"We did too," Ez tells me, touching his own red hair as if making sure it didn't get burned off either. He and Ash are sitting on the wet ground with us. "We ran out after you and when you touched him it stopped."

"Did you feel it?" I ask Venice, pulling him almost roughly against me with the force of my relief. Argos pushes his nose under my armpit, trying to lick Venice's face. "Are you sure you're not hurt?"

"I'm okay, Pen. It's okay. I didn't feel anything."

"It seems like some kind of collective hallucination," Hex says.

"Like a spell," says Ez.

"Spooky," Ash adds.

I let go of Venice and turn to press my cheek against Hex's. "What's happening? I just want things to go back to normal."

"Normal? Never. None of us are normal, Pen. Thank god for that." I can't see his face but I swear I can feel him smile. Then his voice is gruff again. "None of this is normal. You better get used to it. But any problem that comes up, we're going to handle it together, okay?"

Nodding my head, wanting to bury into him. The mud is seeping through my sweatpants and I realize how wet and filthy we all are. A cold white light is trying to break through the clouds. It's officially morning and suddenly I feel exposed, watched.

Ez gets up, then Ash. "Let's go eat," Ez says.

Hex stands and pulls me up with him. Venice lifts Argos in his arms, the dog's muddy paws further staining my brother's T-shirt.

We're all standing there looking toward the horizon and then I remember how this whole thing started. The ship.

I put my hands on Venice's shoulders but he doesn't try to run toward the ship this time. He's just staring at it and his eyes are unreadable.

"What is that?" I say but the last word comes out in a shivering stutter.

"We're not going to find out right now," Hex says. "Let's go inside."

I'm glad to get away from the ship. It could be anything.

There could be Giants out there in the ocean, lying in wait. There could be other humans who might want our food and our water supply. Or the ship could be empty. For some reason this seems just as terrifying and even when I get inside and change into dry clothes I can't stop shivering thinking about what has already happened this morning.

Ez takes a ration of almonds from our stash and roasts apples on the hibachi stove for breakfast. After we've eaten and fed Argos we all gather in the living room and close the curtains so we can't see the ship swaying in the dark waters, as if it's watching us. We try to stay busy with our morning meditation and yoga class, our reading and drawing and repairs—I'm mending some shirts and Venice is attempting to fix a broken chair—but it's like we can't really concentrate. Hex has taken his sword down from the wall above our bed and every so often he reaches for it as if to reassure himself. But we skip sword practice today; it's always hard to get Ez and Ash to comply and Hex, Venice, and I are too worn out from the morning incident to try to convince them. But as the day drawls on I can't sit still anymore.

"We need to do something about it," I say, finally. Before I wanted to get inside the house but now I feel like I'm going crazy just sitting here.

I do a quick checklist of our abilities, trying to see how we could use them against an ominous ship or what might be aboard it. There are Hex's sword-fighting lessons and we regularly lift the weights my father kept in the basement, Ez cooks and guides the meditation and yoga, and Ash's music saved us from being eaten by a Giant. Ash once flew; Ez kept furniture from crushing him during the Earth Shaker; Hex put out fires; Venice once hid himself from the eyes of Giants and he has a supernatural ability with growing plants. And me, I stopped a wall of water from destroying my house during the Earth Shaker and after I lost my eye I began to see random visions of people's pasts, although it's happened much less lately. None of our gifts sound particularly promising.

"I don't want to explore just yet," says Hex. "I don't like the effect it had on Venice."

"But that's the whole point. What if that happens again?"

We all look at Venice but he's busy hammering away at the chair, singing softly to himself. Sometimes he gets a very peaceful look when he's working, as if he's back in our old life, minus the video games. Well, minus just about everything.

Finally he looks up. The peaceful expression is gone. "I won't let it get me again."

"I'm not going," says Ez. "Pen, we just have to wait it out."

I get up and go to the window but I don't open the curtains. "Wait what out? Wait for them to attack?"

"Who's them?" Ez says. "We don't know if anyone's there at all. We don't even know if it's real."

"What, you think it's a figment of all of our imaginations like what happened to Venice's hair?" I say. "Collective post-traumatic stress disorder?"

That's our explanation for almost everything and it kind of makes sense after what we've been through.

"Who knows? It could be anything. We've pretty much seen it all, right?" Ash chimes in.

We pretty much have.

"What do you think, Ven?" I ask, since the rest of them seem to have made up their minds.

My little brother shrugs. "I can beat it now."

"It looked like it was going to burn you to death," I say, which I realize, too late, isn't exactly going to help Venice feel better about what happened. But it might get my friends to change their minds and deal with the situation.

"But it didn't," Hex says. "It was some kind of hallucination we all had at the same time. An"—he pauses and then emphasizes the next word—"illusion. And what's 'it'?

The ship? How do we know they're connected? How do we know it means anything?"

Before I can stop myself I answer. "Because your book says it is. The fire was like what happened to Aeneas's son Ascanius's hair." I pick up Hex's precious *Aeneid*. "It was an omen."

We all look at each other, six sets of somber eyes, including Argos's.

Oh shit, not another prophetic book.

I mean, unless it is a children's picture book about happy and slightly annoying animals or something. Not an epic about omens and wars. We already had to deal with that once, when our lives began to resemble Homer's *Odyssey*.

And I had to bring up *The Aeneid*. Maybe I'm getting as obsessed as Hex is.

"What did the omen in the book mean, though?" Ash asks. "I can't keep track of all your stories."

"You have to start paying attention, man." Hex frowns. "That they should leave and start a civilization of their own. That's the whole point of the book. Be brave, venture forth, make sacrifices."

Ash shakes his dreads as if they'll push the idea out of the room.

"We already have our own civilization, here." Ez puts

his hand on his belly and his face blanches like he's going to be sick.

Or maybe I'm just projecting because that's exactly how I feel. I might be up for exploring the ship after seeing Venice's hair catch on fire but founding civilizations is a whole different thing.

"I'm not going anywhere," Ez continues. "I've had enough of that shit."

"We'll see," says Hex. I know this person: when he says, "We'll see," it means we're going to do exactly what he has planned for us.

In bed that night he tells me he's wiped out from the day even though we didn't do much, really; the incident with the ship has affected all of us. I hold him tighter than usual so that he has to pry my fingers loose from his undershirt in order to shift his position. I close my eyes against the dark, my hand on Hex's heart, and try to match my breathing to his, wishing he were still awake with me.

When I finally fall asleep I dream about my mother again. I'm calling her on the phone, asking her to come home. She says she'll meet me somewhere so I start walking. On the way I pass a graveyard on a hill. I didn't expect it to be there and it disturbs me. It's crowded with bronze and marble statues marking graves, so many that there's nowhere to walk. So many dead, I think, a world of the dead spilling down the sides of the hill. There are androgynous winged figures, women who are turning into trees, males with large heads and torsos balanced precariously on the small, delicate legs of goats, and one statue of the antler man from my other dream. Then I see a statue of my mother. I run to it but it's difficult because of all the statues, all the graves in the way. Some of them are leaning over, threatening to fall on me. I get to the statue but it's not my mother—it's another woman with glittering eyes, and holding a spear. I see the eyes are holes and that there is a fire burning inside of the statue. A liquid substance is beading on her forehead and dripping down her arms. I touch it and see that it's sweat. The statue raises her spear.

I wake shivering in a sheet of my own sweat and call for Hex. He grabs me around the rib cage and holds me until I stop thrashing. I've kicked the covers off and he reaches to retrieve the blanket from the foot of the bed and pull it around us.

"Remember, it's just an illusion," he tells me.

I'm not sure if he means my dream or what happened to my brother. "You want to leave, don't you?" I say into his chest. "Because of the fire. But I thought you didn't believe in illusions."

"I believe in Virgil."

That old man again. "I don't want to leave here. I know we have to at least go to the ship but . . ."

Hex says, "It's okay. I promise, everything will be okay."

"Why?" I ask him. I'm crying, tears running down my face like that sweat dripping off the infernal statue.

"Because I love you," he says. "And that's all we really ever have."

He lifts my face to his and our lips find each other by instinct in the dark. As soon as we kiss my whole body relaxes like I've just been immersed in warm water, in a marble tub with gardenia blossoms floating on it and candles scented with lavender and vanilla burning along the rim. I stretch out so the soles of my feet rest on top of his delicate bony arches and then he flips me over onto my back. He props himself up and leans over me and I cradle his face in my palms. I can feel his hand stroking my throat, moving down to my breasts, massaging them while the other hand supports my neck. Then one finger trails from my solar plexus to my belly, over my pubic bone, between my legs. He pushes my thighs apart with one knee and moves his hand inside of me so I buck up to meet his fingers, coming almost right away. My body is so grateful for him that I want to weep again, but not out of fear now.

"Your turn," I say.

Even after all this time Hex is still shy about letting me give him pleasure. I sit up so we're facing each other cross-legged, holding hands.

"Okay?" I ask. I feel like I always have to check in with him first.

"Okay."

So I push him down on his back and position myself between his legs, my mouth on him, his hands in my hair. He moans, a shudder going through him, and I'm struck by how vulnerable he can be, but only with me, only in our bed.

When he's quiet, he pulls me up to lie on his chest. That heart is beating so fast still. I kiss the *Heartless* tattoo that covers it.

"We're going to explore the ship, aren't we?" I ask him, squinting at the light beginning to creep into the room.

"We received an omen."

Why the hell does he trust that old book by Virgil more than he trusts me? But I brought up the book and it confirms what I know, deep down, we should do. Even the dream about my mother seemed to say to leave home, go find what needs to be found. In *The Aeneid*, Venus appeared to her son Aeneas and told him this very thing.

But the other dream—the one about the fire-eyed, sweating statue—if I relate that to *The Aeneid* it could be read as a warning. Aeneas's people, the Trojans, allowed the wooden horse into their city after they were told about a statue of the goddess Minerva with fire in her eyes and sweat dripping down her body. The Trojans interpreted the statue as a sign and accepted the gift of the horse into the citadel. Obviously that didn't go well since there were Greek soldiers in the horse's belly. Almost everyone was killed except Aeneas and a few others. But ultimately Aeneas had to set forth in spite of the danger.

At least if we go I'll have a chance to utilize all this adrenaline that's been building up in my body since my brother's hair caught on fire. Well, besides what Hex just did with the adrenaline. That helped. That's all I want to think of now.

But Argos's warning bark jars me from the post-lovemaking drowsiness that's overtaken me. Hex is up and holding his sword before I can even consider the reason why our dog is going berserk. I pull my shirt and sweats on and stumble after Hex into the hallway, my single eye adjusting to the sharp light of day.

The man is standing in the kitchen, and Argos has him cornered, a snarling ball of fur and teeth. Argos may be small but when he's protecting us he sounds like a monster, a fearsome beast many times his size with monster young still a-nest.

"Hands up," Hex shouts and instead the man grins, revealing missing teeth, and removes his hood and his broken aviator sunglasses so we can see his eyes.

In spite of the layer of filth, the missing teeth, and the beard he's grown, obscuring most of his face, I recognize him. It's Merk.

Though Merk saved my life more than once, he's still part of the pain.

He was best friends with both my parents but slept with my mother just before she married my dad and got her pregnant with me. My dad accepted me, Merk's child, as his own but banished Merk from our lives. Then Merk went to work for my dad's enemy, Kronen the Giant maker, the mad scientist whose world-ending experiments my father was trying to expose.

Merk must be the one who brings us food and supplies but I still don't fully trust him. Seeing him now it's clear why. He looks like this one actor I remember from Then who played the crazy in all these movies. He had this ragged grin and these eyes that just pinned you down dead-butterfly-under-glass style, and even when he seemed calm you didn't know if he was going to snap and go off on someone, spittle flying.

"What are you doing here?" I ask, pulling my shirt tighter around my body.

"Is that any way to greet your father?" Merk says. His voice is slurred and I wonder if he's drunk. "Your gift horse."

"You scared the shit out of us. Why couldn't you have knocked?"

He raps his knuckles on the kitchen table and Argos lets out a ferocious bark that makes my ears ring. Our little watchdog hasn't really stopped with the low growl this whole time.

"Can you call off the dog, there? Jesus."

I squat down and whistle for Argos to come to me. Ez, Ash, and Venice are in the room with us now. There's a large sack on the floor and our eyes wander to it; we're all wondering if Merk brought us food. I can almost hear the collective growl of our stomachs. Only Hex and Argos don't seem to be thinking about breakfast—they haven't taken their eyes off Merk for a second.

Merk opens the sack and places things on the table—bars of soap, cans of beans, protein bars, jerky, coffee. If you count how Merk has brought me food, you could say he's saved my life more than three times. After the Earth Shaker he came to our house with his men and gave me the keys to a van full of supplies, but it was that one chocolate bar he handed me, when he discovered me in the basement, that I remember most. The sharp snap of the squares and the way they melted into the only sweetness I had left in the world.

I know the pre–Earth Shaker energy bars will taste like rubber and the jerky will be rock hard but I'm grateful for the grams of protein they provide since our diet of fruits and vegetables is lacking. My fingernails snag and peel easily, my hair breaks, and my skin always looks pale.

Hex, Ez, Ash, Venice, and I each eat a protein bar as slowly as we can manage and give Argos a piece of jerky (he doesn't even try to take it slow). Then we all go into the living room where we can see the ship bobbing in the water outside. It reminds me of a hand puppet operated by a drunken puppeteer.

"How fortuitous," Merk says, gnawing on a piece of jerky. His nails are lined with grime and he smells a little like a wet dog. "I came to tell you to leave and here's the way you will."

My pulse accelerates to a hard thumping in my

throat and wrists. What does he mean? After my last journey I vowed never to go away from home again unless I absolutely had to. My friends and brother and I survived the Earth Shaker, the Giants; we've proven ourselves. I don't need any more adventures as long as I live. But then I think again of my dream, my mother telling me to leave.

The Aeneid lies out on a table. Merk taps its cover with his middle finger. "Good book."

"Can you get to the point?" Hex says. "We appreciate the food but why are you really here?"

"Let's head out to that ship tomorrow morning," says Merk, squinting through the window. "I'll tell you there." His eyes looked half crazy before but now there's something else in them that makes my heart feel like a stone sinking into the roiling sea. It's the dark spark of full-fledged madness.

That night I can't sleep, the image of those eyes burning my brain tissue, so I get out of bed and tiptoe to Ez and Ash's room.

"Are you awake?" I ask.

Ez sits up, then Ash, their two heads—one long-haired, one close shorn—silhouetted against the window.

"Not at all," Ash says sleepily.

"Can I come in with you?"

Ash pats the bed and I hop in between them. It's too warm and smells of sleep but I don't mind; I'm glad to have their company. "Hex went to sleep in, like, two seconds," I say. "He loves this adventure shit. It's Ambien for him or something."

Ez shnuzzles down beside me. "Not me."

"Why'd you have to bring up that book? He's addicted to it," Ash says. I don't admit it, but I'm becoming more than a little preoccupied with *The Aeneid* too. "And by the way, I'm not up to founding a new civilization anytime soon."

"I'm just glad he isn't reading *The Iliad*. It's *all* about the wars."

"We better confiscate the shelves."

"Only pretty, dreamy books," Ez says.

Ash agrees. "Tell us a story tonight, Pen. We need one."

"I don't know," I say. "I haven't been feeling very inspired."

"It's better than having to carry a weapon and check out some weird old ship," says Ez.

"Good point."

Ash puts his arm around my shoulder. "I'll sing to give you some inspiration." His voice is as angelic as if it really did come from the throat of the winged creature in

Ez's painting and as I sit back and close my eyes it takes me away.

※ ❦ ※

An island with black quartz sand glittering down to the sea. Tall trees grow just up from the beach. The sky is a blue we haven't seen since before the Earth Shaker. In the distance is a building gleaming as if it's made of semiprecious stone.

But something is happening.

Now the sky is filled with lethal black smoke and the trees have fallen, felled by some great storm.

※ ❦ ※

I've never smelled anything in my visions before but this time I reach to cover my nose and mouth from the imagined stench. Something is very wrong here.

I remember what Venice said about stories helping us envision the action we should take. But it doesn't seem like this vision will help my friends, who only want to sleep well tonight. And it certainly won't help me. So I just tell Ez and Ash about the first part of what I saw— the blue sky, the sunshine, the quartz palace. I fill it with silken dresses, mythic-themed paintings, goblets of nectar, and plates of figs, cheeses, and cakes. I make the floors inlaid stone depicting roses and suns and moons

⌐ 38 ⌐

and eyes. I give myself my missing eye back and I add someone else, a pale, muscular man with a crown made of antlers like the man in my last two dreams.

"He sounds dreamy," Ez says.

Ash playfully slugs him. "What's this place called?"

"The Island," I say, without thinking. "The Island of Excess Love."

3

THE TROJAN HORSE

WE STAND AT THE SHORE, Venice holding Argos, and Ash, Ez, and me armed with knives. Hex with his sword. Merk has a rifle. I'm not a fan of guns in the hands of men with crazed eyes and I sort of wish he'd left it behind. I think about those schoolchildren that madman killed back Then. Just marched into the school and shot them multiple times. This world seems insane but in some ways it's not that much different from before the Earth Shaker. The day of that shooting I thought the end of the world had come. So it's no surprise we're all where we are now.

But Merk's gun was the thing that convinced Ez and Ash it was safe enough to explore the ship, and as anxious as I am, I know it's better to understand what we're dealing with.

Up close I can see that on the prow is a wooden figurehead of a rearing horse, eyes rolling in its head and mouth open so you can see its carved teeth. If this were a carousel horse it would have to be removed to keep from scaring the children.

And it reminds me of something else.

"The Trojan horse," Hex says.

"Not such a great sign," I tell him. "If we're looking to ancient Greek and Roman texts for prophecy."

"Depends on whose side you're on."

But none of this matters because we are now all walking toward the black-slicked rocks against which the ship is moored. It's like I can't turn back even if I wanted to. Salt water sprays my face but I don't taste it with my tongue the way I would have in the past; instead I wipe it off with the back of my sleeve. Who knows what contaminants are in these waters? That's why we rarely come down here and we haven't even tried to fish. But now, for some reason I don't understand, in spite of what happened to the Trojans, I feel compelled to board this ship.

Merk boards first, whistling through his teeth like a pirate, merrily walking the plank, then Hex; then Ash, Ez, me, and Venice.

As soon as I step onto the deck I feel a quickening in my body. I stare up at the sails hanging from the masts. They look ghostly, animated by the wind against the gray sky. The scent of brine prickles my nostrils and I can feel the vibration of Hex's and Merk's boots on the wood slats of the deck as my father and lover go to opposite sides of the ship.

A low rumbling growl comes from Argos's throat as soon as Venice is behind me. Argos twists himself in Ven's arms—head one way, body another, eyes rolling into whiteness as if he's possessed—and Venice has to grab him against his chest to keep him from going overboard.

"It's okay, boy. It's okay." But Venice's voice sounds very thin and frightened against the rush of the wind. I want to go to help him but instead I just stand there, staring at Hex, who is putting his hands on the carved wooden wheel that steers the ship.

"Helm," he says, to no one in particular. He surveys other parts of the boat around him. "Jib. Mast. Poop deck. Stern. The keel's over there." Of course Hex knows about sailing. He told us he used to take lessons when he was a kid. Encyclopedia fanatic that I am, I've learned these parts before, although I don't know how to sail. I'm relieved that this ship is so big because even if we were experienced sailors we'd never be able to manage it; we'd have to stay home.

Ez is hovering about like a worried grandpa wringing his hands. I think he's crying. Ash is singing in a high strained voice—a lamentation about a terrible storm. Venice is still struggling with Argos, whose barks are getting louder. Merk is stalking around with his gun.

Without waiting for Merk or Hex to lead the way, I feel for my knife in my pocket and go down through the hatch into the cabin. It's wood paneled with hammocks swinging from the low ceiling and bunks that remind me of coffins. A wooden table by a wood-burning stove. I have a sudden memory of a video about a warship, a brig, I saw on YouTube once where the ship doctor had to perform surgery on injured crew members on the captain's dining table. To distract myself from this thought I peer inside the cupboards—they're fully stocked with canned goods and bottles of wine. But this is weird too; what happened to the crew of this ship? The air smells musty and there's a layer of dust furring everything.

Hex comes down into the cabin and I imagine he's here to make sure I'm all right but when I say his name he just walks away. Why? I want to go after him but it suddenly feels like I can't. He is going into the shadows and I can't see him anymore. I try to call his name again but this time no words come out. It's like those dreams where you're debilitated; you can't run, you can't scream. But I don't need to scream, do I? I look around and suddenly I don't recognize where I am. Did I move? Where is the way back up to the deck? I sit down on the cabin floor because I can't walk anymore. The linoleum is stained and peeling. I'm trying to remember what I must do, where I need to go. There's someone I have to speak to. . . . The only name that comes to me is Venice. I can't call for him but I must. A phone number beeps itself out in my head but I don't know whose it is. And there aren't any phones anymore, right? Someone comes down through the hatch and sits beside me. It's Ez.

"Eliot?" he says.

I look at his face and it is long and twisted, his mouth a grimace, his eyes blanked out with pain.

"Eliot, I thought you were dead," Ez says. "You're dead. You look dead."

Eliot is Ez's twin brother who died in the Earth Shaker. Does Ez think I'm him? I can't help Ez; there's nothing I can say, no words. I need him to make this thing stop that's happening. I want to tell him that what he sees isn't real, tell him something that has to do with Ash or Hex, or maybe Venice, but I can't speak. And what did I want to say? And where is Hex? He could be anywhere. Who did this to us? I want to know what's happening but I can't ask. I reach for Ez's arm but he feels insubstantial, just stares at my hand on his bicep like it's a foreign object. I think someone has done something to us but I don't know who or what.

Kronen, the Giant maker, is standing there behind the table. He's holding up a large glass tumbler and shaking it. Inside are round, gelatinous things that jiggle in some sort of brine. Eyeballs. I touch my patch. It's not here. Where is it? Will someone see my empty socket? I cringe against the bunk behind me. Ez has gone. I want to cry for Hex but I still can't speak. I want this to stop but how do you make it stop?

Ash is lying on his back on the wooden table. "Don't touch me," he whispers. "Just because I don't have anywhere to go doesn't mean you can touch me like that."

Kronen is gone. Is Ash talking to me?

He turns his head and stares down at me, his green-jade eyes framed with eyelashes that look as if he's curled them. "You took me in when my mom called me a faggot. I trusted you. I didn't think you would do that."

"Who do you think I am?" I ask.

He sits up on the table and points his finger at me. "You raped me! I was just a kid. You said it was my fault for coming to you like that, for singing to you and looking at you like that. It wasn't my fault."

Ash gets up from the table and pushes me so hard that I fall backwards onto the floor. I cover my head with my hands and listen as he walks away. I'm afraid Kronen will come back and take my other eye so I try to hide under the table.

When I glance up Hex is staring at me, his face coming in and out of focus, his eyes huge and black. "You look like shit," he snarls.

Why would Hex say something like that to me? I want to tell him that it's mean, but I can't talk.

"You think it's acceptable parenting to get high like that? In front of your kid?"

His mother? I wonder. Am I Hex's mother? Am I high? I didn't take anything, did I? Where is Kronen? If he takes my other eye I will not see.

"I'm sorry," I say to Hex. Each word feels like a huge rock I have to lift but I'm determined to speak, even if it kills me. "I'm sorry, baby. I didn't mean to hurt you."

We hear screaming from above deck and Hex grabs me by the arm until I'm standing, leaning against him. The cabin is spinning. I need to lie down but Kronen will come back, get me, and cut out my eye.

Hex pulls me up through the hatch. Night has come and a cold wind goes through my body like I don't exist. How did that much time pass?

I see Argos tied up, still barking. Merk is pointing his gun at something I can't make out.

Venice is walking toward Merk, speaking softly.

Get away! The words shriek in my head but I can't sound them out. I grip Hex's arm; he ignores me.

"Motherfucking snakes. I'll blow your goddamn brains out," Merk says to the air.

"Do you see snakes?" Venice asks.

"Sea snakes. Two of them. They want to strangle the shit out of me," Merk tells him, bringing the gun to eye level and taking aim.

"They can't hurt you," Venice says. "I promise."

Merk whirls around, pointing the gun, and I have to hold on to the side of the ship to keep from collapsing to the deck. "Motherfucker snakes!" he yells at me.

Venice runs to me, blocking me with his body. "It's the ship. It's bewitched," he says. "We have to get off."

"I'm not going anywhere. The snakes will kill us all," Merk says and fires a shot. The whole world goes silent, even the waves. I dive down to the deck, pulling Venice with me.

When I realize I'm not dead I open my eyes; I'm still clinging to my brother's shirt. He gently pushes me off of him. "It's okay, Pen, I'll take care of it. It's okay." Then he stands again and yells, "Merk! There aren't any snakes. You almost shot at your daughter. We have to get off this ship. We're under some kind of spell."

Merk stares out at the water. "Serpents of hell." He lifts his ragged face to the night sky.

"We need to leave," Venice says. "You killed the snakes, Merk. Now we can leave."

Merk points up. We all look. Something bright arcs across the firmament, over our heads.

"A shooting star," Merk says. "A sign. It's a sign! Like from that book. That book you have at home. Even the survival of that book is a sign. We must take a journey to find the new world!" He turns to me, pointing his finger. "You are the founder of the new world! You! It has been prophesied."

"Yes, sure, okay," Venice says. "But we have to get supplies first. We have to get off this ship, okay?" He enunciates each word as if speaking to a child.

Merk slumps down to the deck and holds his head. "Grace!" he cries. "Grace, forgive me."

"She wants you to leave," says Venice. "We all have to leave, okay? Come on, Pen. Hex. Ez. Ash." Saying our names as if he's trying to help us recall who we are. He doesn't say Kronen's name. I touch my empty socket.

I must have said his name because Venice says, "He's dead, Pen. That man is dead. You killed him."

"Tell us the story of how you killed him?" He turns to Ash and Ez who've joined us. "Sing us the story, Ash.

Remember how Pen killed Kronen?" Digging in his pocket he pulls out a small piece of chalk. "I bet you could draw it, Ez. How Pen killed Kronen? You can do it."

Ez, Ash, and I all stare at each other. Then Ash closes his eyes, takes a deep breath as if about to throw himself into battle, and begins to sing. The music floats over me like a dark vapor. I can't really make out the words but the sounds form images in my mind—a man in a jacket made of dried skin with a Giant of his own creation looming behind him. My hands holding a sword. *You killed Kronen. He's dead. From this you are safe.*

Ez grabs the chalk from Venice, gets on his knees, and begins to scribble all over the boat's deck. The images he draws are the same ones I see in my mind.

"I killed Kronen," I say.

"Yes, Pen. That was real. What you've seen here isn't real."

I don't know how my little brother gets us all off of the demon ship full of the dead but I know it has something to do with our stories, pictures, and songs. All I remember next is being back in the pink house with tears from my unstolen eye wet on my face.

4

PEN'S DESTINY

WE GATHER IN THE LIVING ROOM and eat some canned minestrone soup Merk brought; no one is up to picking fresh vegetables tonight. My head hurts, like my brain is swollen, edema, pressing against my skull. Venice found another patch to cover my eye.

It's Hex who speaks first, rubbing his temples; I guess he feels like I do. "What the hell was that?"

Merk focuses his eyes on my brother, who flinches a little. "Why didn't it get you?"

"I have no idea."

"There's something special about that kid." Merk slurps down some soup and scowls out the window. "He'll be helpful when we go back out."

Hex almost jumps out of his chair. "What the fuck are you talking about? We're not going near that ship again. If anything, we'll set fire to it."

"How else will we get to the new world?" Merk replies, very calm. He wipes his nose on his filthy sleeve.

"That thing almost killed us," Hex growls; he sounds like Argos. "*You* almost killed us with that gun. And the six of us couldn't man that ship even if it wasn't bewitched."

Merk stands and goes to the window. He puts both hands on the glass, leaving greasy smudges. "The ghosts will sail us there," he says.

He's gone over the edge for sure this time.

"You need to rest," I tell him. "Why don't you lie down?"

Merk turns and saunters out of the room like an old-time cowboy. First a pirate, now this. He really missed his calling as an actor but it's too late for that now. "Wait and see," he says over his shoulder. "We will board that ship again and the ghosts will sail us to the new world. Pen will be the founder of a civilization. It is her destiny. The star spoke it. As her father, I must accompany her."

I think about the shooting star we saw. Though I was too out of it at the time to realize, Merk interpreted the star as another omen. In *The Aeneid* it was a sign that Aeneas's father Anchises should join Aeneas on his journey. Merk certainly sees the star as a reason to go.

I look over at Hex, wanting to touch him but I'm not sure if we're okay. The venom with which he spoke to me on the ship still scares me, even if he thought I was his mother at the time.

"I thought Luther was there," Ash says. Luther is the choral director Ash lived with when his mom threw him out for being gay. Luther the pedophile, the one Ash thought I was when we were under the ship's spell. Why did they all think I was someone they hated? The question makes me cold from my skin to my insides, as if I'm still out in the wind.

"I thought I saw my mother." I wonder if Hex is avoiding eye contact on purpose when he says this.

"Pen thought she saw Kronen," says Venice. "And Merk thought it was sea snakes that wanted to kill him."

Like the sea snakes in *The Aeneid* that killed the Trojan Laocoön and his two young sons, when Laocoön tried to convince them not to take the Trojan horse in through the gates. Once again there are parallels with the epic but none of it makes any real sense in this mad world.

Hex rolls his eyes. "Figures he'd be the one to see the snakes. He's fucking insane even without a spell."

"But Ez saw Eliot," I say. "Not someone he hates, obviously. Why was that?"

"Why did he leave me?" Ez says under his breath.

"Sometimes when I'm not thinking clearly I hate him for dying. He should be with us." His eyes are still red. I go and put my arm around his shoulders; he feels thinner than usual.

"Well, we're not going back out there," says Venice. "We may have to burn it like Hex said."

I've never heard my brother sound so assertive, as if the experience on the ship changed him, let him see that in some way he is stronger than all of us. Hex is looking at him differently, too. Not as a child but as a peer.

"I'm not going near it," Ez says. "I told you to stay away from it and you didn't listen." His voice has risen in pitch and I see Hex's eyes get bigger and his lips tighten like they're on a drawstring.

"This is all bullshit," he says. "I need to go meditate."

I start to join him but something in his face tells me not to and I go to the window instead. I can see the wooden horse rear up on the prow of the ship as it moves in the water.

Hex seems to be avoiding me all night. When he finally comes to bed I feel an exhale of relief move through my whole body. But he turns his face to the wall. I ask him what's wrong.

"I don't want to talk about it," he says. "Can we just not talk for once?"

I can't not talk. And since when doesn't Hex want to talk to me? "Why did you think I was your mother?" I say, in spite of myself.

He sits up in bed and glares at me. "Why do you think? I was fucked up. I might as well have been high."

"Is that what this is about? You think you got high again? It wasn't anyone's fault. We didn't know this would happen."

"That's not the point. I don't like being out of control."

But Hex, I think, *we're always out of control. Look around you.*

"Your mother was out of control," I say instead. "But you're not her. And neither am I." Hex has told me that his mother would leave him alone all the time when he was little and that when she was home she was so drunk or high she hardly knew who he was. She had black hair and green eyes and pale skin like Hex's; I saw a vision of her once, staggering around the house in a silk nightgown with a bottle of liquor, reciting Shakespeare. He hated her. I remember the way he looked at me on the ship, like he wanted to harm me. It's hard to forget that look, even if he didn't realize it was me.

"Just go to sleep," he says, as if he still doesn't know who I am.

We wake to a shaking and I think, This is it again, another Earth Shaker. Another one. It's here.

The whole house is moving and then I hear Venice call out.

"Giant!"

It's not just a nightmare. As I run downstairs I can see the Giant coming toward us through the window. He staggers blind, his hands out in front of him. He's sniffing the air, like he's tracking me, my scent, no one else's. I'm the one who blinded him and killed his father.

My hair stands up on my head; my voice catches in my throat.

I don't remember how my friends and my brother and dog and I get out of the house but somehow we are outside in the mournful gray dawn and Bull is still coming toward us. I grab Venice's hand. He has Argos, and Hex and Ez and Ash are with us and we are running through the mud.

We are running toward the ship because there's nowhere else to go, or at least that's what the ship is telling us, calling us to it, beckoning us back. The horse on the prow rears out of the water, sea foam frothing from its mouth like the beast has gone mad.

Where's Merk? I think but it's too late and I'm at the ship and climbing the rocks, clambering over the side onto the deck.

Ghosts, Merk said.

I hear a shot and turn around and there's Merk, running toward us, backwards, shooting his rifle at Bull but Bull keeps coming. How will we ever sail this ship? There's no way—there are only six of us.

And then, before I can think anything else, the Giant, Bull, is at the shore, his hand reaching out, the warts bubbling up on his hand, the smell of his breath like rotten fish, like he's swallowed a whole school of foul fish. And then the ship is sailing, as if on its own, away from our home and toward my unwanted destiny.

5

THE GHOST SHIP SAILS

THE SHIP IS MOVING through the water, manned
by ghosts.

How else could it be moving? I am too dizzy and weak
and confused and bewitched to question it. I'm staring
at Merk who is standing in front of me with a gun in one
hand and a length of rope coiled over his arm. I don't
know when he got the rope.

"Down you go, mateys," he says. "I'll tie you up and
stow you below until we reach our destination. Can't
have you harming one another." Since when is he a pirate? He grins and I see the missing teeth.

"Fuck off," Hex says. "We're not going anywhere.
You're not in charge."

I hadn't noticed that Hex was right behind me. I try to say something to him but I can't.

"It's for your own good," Merk says to Hex. "Now come right over here like a good girl."

Even in my confusion I know that's not the thing to say to Hex, who is not what he once was. He lunges at Merk and Merk fires the gun and I scream, the fear tearing through my spell-induced muteness. Hex dives to the deck and Merk grabs him and wrestles him and I throw myself onto Merk.

Then there is a loud sharp sound and pain and then everything is dark.

When I open my eyes I am lying in darkness, tied up. The rope is abrading my wrists and blood is pounding in my skull. The boat is moving beneath me, the air is dank, and my stomach wobbles like a jellyfish. Once when walking on the beach, one stung me on my foot and the pain had the same gelatinous, veined quality as the creature that administered it.

"Hex!" I manage to say, after a long time, the muteness trying to strangle me again.

Someone is speaking to me but I can't see who it is. "Pen, listen to me very carefully. We're back on the ship.

You're under some kind of spell. Your father Merk is under it too. He tied us all up. I don't know where Hex is, or Ash or Ez. Or Argos. I think Merk tied them up too. But I think everything is going to be okay. We just have to be patient."

"Who are you?" I ask. "Are you a ghost?"

"I'm your brother, Venice."

"I don't know who you are," I whisper. I think the ghost might want to harm me.

"I'll tell you," he says. "Don't be afraid."

When he finishes telling me the story about the family ripped apart by an earthquake, the ghost pauses as if trying to catch his breath. Or hold back a sob.

Is he a ghost? Ghosts don't breathe. Ghosts don't cry.

But whoever he is, my heart leaps toward the picture he's painted in my brain—a three-story house the color of pink roses, full of food and music and love. I want to go there, that's all I want.

"Just don't be afraid, okay?" he tells me. "You are very brave."

I don't know what to say. I am afraid. I'm afraid of everything. When he says the word *brave*, he must not be talking about me.

"The spell only seems to work on the ship. When we reach land you'll be yourself again."

Reach land? What land? Even in this confused state I know I have to get back to the house he told me about. "I want to go home."

"I know," he says. "But I think there must be some reason why we have to go wherever this ship is taking us. Maybe someone needs help."

I don't know how to help anyone, not even myself. "Why aren't you . . ." I try to ask but my tongue feels thick.

"Why aren't I under the spell? I don't know. It didn't affect me."

My stomach interrupts us with a loud growl. "Are you hungry?" the ghost asks.

I tell him that I am, and thirsty, too. My mouth feels like sand and salt.

"Merk will bring us food and water," the ghost, my brother, promises. But I don't know what I believe anymore.

And then I see the man who took my eye.

He's standing above me wearing a black top hat and a long black coat that resembles charred skin. On his hands are thick black rubber gloves and on his feet are heavy boots with sharp spikes. His eyes are hidden behind dark oversize goggles. He takes out something from the pocket of his coat and fondles it in his gloved hand.

Then he removes the goggles and smiles at me, his face stretching into a long, strange shape like a child's Halloween mask. One eye is an empty hollow. Like mine. The man takes the thing from his pocket, holding it tenderly between his thumb and forefinger, and pushes it into the eye socket. It's brown and smaller than his other eye and I know where he got it. It's mine.

"Are you okay?" the ghost says. I'd forgotten he was there.

I can't speak so I just point at the man.

"Do you see someone who scares you? A dark-haired man with a small beard?"

"Yes," I manage.

"He's dead," the ghost promises me. "I'll tell you a story, okay?"

"My eye," I say.

"That's Kronen. The Giant maker."

The ghost pauses as if to gauge my reaction and then goes on in a soft voice. I try to listen to him but I'm still staring at Kronen who is doing a slow jig in his heavy boots, his face twisted into that grimacing smile.

"You killed him. You're having a different kind of vision now, but it's not real. It's because we're on the ship. It makes you see things that frighten you. Tell Kronen to leave you alone. You've already killed him."

Kronen leans close to me so I can see my eye stuck in his misshapen head.

"Tell him," my ghost brother says.

I can't.

"Tell him."

"Venice?"

"Yes, I'm Venice. You can tell him."

I see a tall gold building made of the skeletons of the dead. BANK OF THE APOCALYPSE, reads a sign. A man and a Giant stand before me. Kronen and Kutter. I'm holding a sword in my hand. Hex's sword. He is gone but I'll find him again. I will find him, and my other friends.

And the words come to me then. "I know of many things," I say. "Gods and monsters, transformations, spells and enchantments, trees and oceans, hospitality, loyalty, betrayal, great wars. I know of *kleos*—glory—and I know of love."

"You are Pen the storyteller," says my brother, Venice, the ghost. "Your words are powerful. Your love is powerful."

And with that Kronen fades away into the bowels of the ship.

6

MAELSTROM

I'M SAFE FROM THE MONSTER maker Kronen but I'm not safe from the monsters of thirst and hunger. My lips are ringed with sore, dry skin that gets more irritated when I probe it with my swollen tongue. The roof of my mouth is swollen, too, and it even hurts to blink my eyes. My stomach seethes.

Venice keeps talking to me in his soothing ghost voice but he sounds farther and farther away.

At last we hear footsteps and someone is here with us.

The man holds my head up and pours fresh water into my mouth, relieving the dirty thirst. I try not to let a single drop escape even though he's pouring too fast and I have to keep swallowing hard. Then he feeds me some type of porridge with a spoon. I gulp it down as fast as he'll give it to me.

"Good job, girl, we'll be at our destination soon," the man growls.

When he leaves, ghost boy tells me the man's name is Merk and that he's my father. But he can't be. I remember my father. He was a tall, quiet man with gentle hands, not this frightening pirate who has tied us up in the hull of a haunted ship.

"Why?" I ask, yearning for my real father, my real life, not this.

"Why what?"

"Why everything? Why are we here? Where is here? What happened to everyone?" I don't want to cry but I can feel a tingling in my tear ducts.

"Please try to rest now," he says. So I close my eyes, hoping it will all be different when I wake up. Hoping I will be home, wherever that is, locked in safely, away from the world.

Instead I wake to a violent swaying. The ship is being tossed as if spewed between the maws of two blue sea monsters and we can hear the wind thrashing above us.

"It's just a storm," Venice says.

Just a storm? This isn't any regular storm. A word from a book comes to my mind, a word from a book someone I love read to me. *Maelstrom.*

My stomach lurches and I pray that I won't vomit the food that man gave me earlier.

"Just try to breathe," Venice tells me. "Like Hex and Ez taught us. Remember?"

It's almost worse to think about breathing. What if I've forgotten how to breathe at all? What if some part of my brain has been permanently damaged so it will always feel like I have to consciously control every blink and breath?

While I'm gulping air we hear a door bang open and shouting and stomping and bumping and then three other figures, also trussed up with rope, are here in the dark with us.

I can't see their faces. One of them is sobbing, one of them is singing paeans like an angel, and the third is screaming obscenities while Venice tries to quiet them down.

"What the fuck?" the swearing one says.

"Hex, try to stay calm. There's a storm but I think it will be okay. We have to keep it together."

Hex? Hex is here?

"Fuck that! And who's crying? Shut the fuck up with the crying, will you?"

That doesn't sound like Hex.

The crying one makes shuddering, gulping sounds as he tries to stifle his sobs.

"Ez, it's okay," Venice says. "We'll be okay."

"Eliot?" says the crying one.

"No, it's Venice, Pen's brother."

"Where's my brother?"

"Ez, listen carefully, Eliot isn't here. You are all under some kind of a spell. But I think when we can get off the ship it will stop."

The singing one starts up again. Maybe he is an angel. The sound is celestial—if it were a color it would be pale blue—but the ship is rocking so hard I can't really appreciate it. It's like hearing angels sing when you're tied up in hell. I go back to concentrating on not throwing up.

"Shut the fuck up, everyone! Stop singing!" The swearer.

"Ash, can you be quiet for a little while?" Venice says gently, which seems to be the only tone he ever uses. Maybe that's a ghost thing. "It's really nice but everyone's having a hard time right now."

The ship heaves and one of the bodies rolls closer to me and I can see his black hair, the white ovoid of his face. My heart strains against the rope around my chest.

"What's wrong with you?" he practically spits. "Your

eyes look crazy. Are you high? I told you not to get high anymore. You are such a mess."

"Hex," says Venice. "That's Pen, your girlfriend. Do you remember her?"

"Bitch," Hex mutters.

My stomach is working its way up to my mouth and I'm bathed in the cold sweat of nausea. The ghost boy wriggles closer so our shoulders are touching. "He doesn't know who you are," he says. "Do you know who he is?"

I remember a slim, black-haired person holding me in a bed, reading me stories while the world went to hell around us. But we were safe; we had each other. He would never have called me a bitch. He loved me, didn't he? He . . .

The ship seizes again and the porridge erupts, splashing out of me in a puddle of stench.

"You're disgusting," he says, like he's pumping me with venom, and it feels as if I might as well have disgorged my own heart.

I don't understand why we were forced away from our home. For what? For this?

"Talk to him," my little ghost brother tells me. "Tell him who you are."

The singing and crying are louder now. I'm too sick to do anything. "I want to go home."

"I know. But we can't now. Tell him about you."

"Hex?" I try. "It's me, Pen."

He doesn't answer.

So I try harder, because that's all you can do, isn't it? I try to breathe and focus and follow the pictures in my mind, letting them lead me. "Do you remember? We, and our friends, fought Giants and witches and in the end we lost each other but finally we were reunited. You came back to me. We love each other," I say. "I love you."

I wait, expecting him to curse at me, but he's silent. So are Ash and Ez. Even the ship holds its breath. But by now I should know the sound of silence before an eruption.

Something crashes and bangs, slamming us against the side of the ship, and just as Hex says my name, his voice different this time (perhaps with the dawning of recognition?), I am lost once again in darkness.

7

CADAVERS

WHEN I WAKE I'M LYING on wet black sand. It glints—shattered quartz crystal—in the sunlight that warms my back. Sunlight? Pure and bright the way it was, Then. The color of yellow crocuses. I dig my hands into the sand, rubbing the grains between my fingers. I try to sit up but my body is too sore and weak. My hair is heavy and, when I touch it, it's matted with strands of seaweed and bits of broken shells. There's a crusty patch of dried blood on my left temple, which accounts for the pain in my head.

I try to piece everything together in my mind, like when you wake up from a nightmare that you want to make sense of, a nightmare of sea monsters, of no lesser ilk than Scylla and Charybdis, but this is real. I am Pen. Penelope Overland. The Earth Shaker changed everything but I still live in a pink house by the sea. A Giant chased me and my family and friends onto a bewitched ship. It sailed us out into the waters and Merk, my birth father, also bewitched, tied us up and threw us into the lower compartment. Hex couldn't remember who I was. He seemed to hate me. I tried to explain. There was a storm. . . .

Oh, god, Hex. Ez. Ash. Venice. Argos. Even Merk's gone. And there is no sign of our ship with the portentous horse on its prow.

I force myself to sit up and look around me. I'm on a beach, in a cove. Clear blue water slides up onto the sand and then retreats. A forest of trees rises in the distance. Yellow, white, and purple wildflowers and tall sea grasses grow down toward the shore. I may be dreaming but I think I can hear bird songs.

Above me fly a flock of white birds. Doves? I can count twelve. There was a dove in the dream I had about my mother. In *The Aeneid* two doves sent by Venus led Aeneas to the golden bough, the enchanted branch he had to give to Proserpina, queen of the underworld, in order to be admitted to her realm to visit the shade of his dead father. So the sighting of these birds is especially significant (though I'm not exactly sure in what way), but any bird sighting would be.

It's like a world before the Earth Shaker hit.

But none of it will matter without the people I love.

I call their names, one by one, but there is no answer. I stagger to my feet, dragging my sodden limbs across the sand. In the distance I see a dark shape lying prone. I don't want to see. I don't want to go over to it.

But of course I do.

It's Hex. He's flat on his back with his eyes closed and his mouth open. I throw myself on top of him and put my head to his bare, tattooed chest. I put my hands over his heart, fasten my lips to his, and try to remember how to give mouth-to-mouth. He is still. And cold. And paler than pale. I scream his name.

And then I feel a hand on my shoulder and I look up and he is standing over me, staring down at me. And at himself.

"I'm here. Pen? I thought you were . . . Pen?" Hex, who never cries, has tears in his eyes. "Are you okay? Your head was bleeding."

"I'm okay. You're here."

He falls to his knees beside me and we embrace, his warm skin crusted with dirt and salt. I'm never going to let go of him.

When we finally pull apart and look around us, the island swept with sunshine and birdsong gives me chills. Dead Hex still lies at my feet. Another hallucination? Or is this live one a figment of my imagination? No, I'm sure he's real, though I can't explain how I know.

"Where are the others?" I say.

"I don't know, baby. There must have been a ship-wreck. But we're here so it couldn't have been too bad. We'll look for them. I have to show you something first."

"No, we have to . . ."

"It won't take long. You need to see."

He takes my hand and leads me up the beach to where another body is lying. A girl with long, bony limbs and ragged hair. We kneel beside her and Hex untangles the fishing net caught around her legs and brushes sand off of her face with his fingertips.

She stares at us, with darkling eyes.

I gasp.

She's me.

"Why?" I ask no one. I should know by now that there is no answer to *why*. Then I start screaming again, call-ing for Ez and Ash and Argos and especially for Venice. I can remember how he talked to me on the ship, helping me navigate the madness that had taken over. Merk had tied us up. I don't scream for Merk.

Hex takes me by both shoulders and makes me look at him. "We have to stay calm," he says. "Okay?"

I nod, staring out at the water. The waves seem benign, sparking in the sunshine. I'm not used to the sight of sun on waves; the sea at home is dark as lead in the gray light. I stare, mesmerized by it. I'd forgotten how wondrous the world could be but it still doesn't make up for the fact that the rest of my loved ones are gone.

"Let's start over there, Pen, among the trees, okay? We need to find fresh water before we do anything."

So I pull my gaze away from the waves and we go toward the trees with peeling red and green bark and shiny dark green leaves, seeking water we can drink. I hadn't noticed how thirsty I was. The sun felt good on my skin at first but my shoulders are turning red and the shade of the trees is welcome. The air smells moist and sweet and it doesn't take us long to find a small creek with blackberries growing on its banks. Hex examines the berries and when we're pretty sure they're safe we eat them by the finger-staining handful and wash them down with the creek water. It's clear and bright and refreshes us instantly. Something flashes by. A fish, which means there's definitely animal life here, probably untainted, by the looks of it, and maybe no serious predators (meaning Giants), although that might be wishful thinking.

As we're heading back toward the beach through the grove we see what appear to be two holes recently dug in the ground.

"They look like graves," Hex says.

We stop and stare at each other. Graves? For our corpses lying on the beach? Are we meant to bury ourselves? Of all the things I've been required to do, this may be the strangest. The only reason I even consider this task, though, is that I don't really want to look for the corpses of my friends and family back on the beach. What if we find their dead bodies? Even if it's a wickedy spell, we might think it's real. I'm relieved that at least there are only two graves here.

Hex and I go back to my body and lift it carefully. We carry it back up the beach to the trees. It feels small and stiff in my arms, and I remember carrying my mother's body when I found her in Las Vegas just before she died. I can't look at this corpse's face.

Hex speaks to me softly the whole way. "I don't understand this, Pen, but it seems like what we're supposed to do, don't you think? Like, let's pretend we're in a story or a dream. In the epics the burial of the dead is a very important, sacred thing."

But even in The Aeneid they didn't have to bury themselves.

We lay my body in the grave and go back to get Hex.

He doesn't weigh much more than I do. I try to keep my eyes on the live Hex as we carry the dead one to his final resting place. The two dead versions of us lie there and I don't feel like crying; I don't feel anything, except the same desire to get out of here and go home. What kind of spell is this? What weird magic? And what is it supposed to be telling us? That we must leave our old selves behind? What are we meant to learn from it all?

We shove dirt over our corpses and pat it down and then Hex breaks off sprigs, from a bush covered in white flowers that look like the lace of a bridal dress, and sticks one on top of each mound.

"What should I say?" he asks.

"Here lie Hex and Pen, warriors, storytellers, survivors, friends, and lovers. May their souls be reborn to do good and restore this planet," I say, surprising myself. Since when do I hope to restore this planet? It's too big a task, and now Venice and Ez and Ash are gone. If we don't find them I'll be lucky if I can restore my own heart.

Hex takes my hand and we run back to the beach. We go down to the water and search among the rocks. Something is lodged in the sand and I recognize the open mouth and staring eyes of the wooden horse from our ship's prow. Severed like this it resembles the skull of an actual horse. That doesn't bode well. There must have been a serious shipwreck.

I put my face in my hands, wanting to make all of this go away. "How do we not give up?"

"Because we have no other choice?"

In the dark space between my palms I see colors emerge and then shatter into fragments like bits of stained glass. Then the colors re-form into images. I see Venice holding Argos, standing with Ez and Ash. They are in a room where waterfalls splash down rock walls into shallow pools. Ash is singing and Ez is sketching. A young man is seated on a flower-covered dais in front of my brother and my friends. The smoke of incense partially occludes him but I see that his eyes are wide spaced, pale, and strange. He wears a crown of antlers, decorated with flowers, on his head.

"They're okay," I say. "Hex, they're okay. I see them." Usually my visions are of the more distant past but I'm pretty sure this one is something that just happened. Weirdly, the man looks like the one in the vision I had of the black quartz island.

I describe what I've seen to Hex.

He puts his arm around my shoulder. He doesn't question these things.

"Can you tell where?"

I shake my head, no. The vision is gone.

"Let's get some more to eat, and some rest," Hex says. "Then we'll look for them."

He and I head back to the stream with the fishing net we removed from my corpse. Hex holds it; I don't like the idea of touching something that was wrapped around my dead body.

We stand in the water and Hex swishes the net around; it's easy to catch fish. They're small and silvery and, I think, more trusting than they should be. Hex rubs two sticks together to ignite a spark and builds a fire. Then we clean and cook the fish on sticks and eat them. I'm not disgusted at all, although I never liked the idea of killing and eating an animal before. Hunger wins every battle, though. The fish taste fresh, moist, and clean.

"We should bathe now," Hex suggests. He pulls off his shirt and jeans and slips into the deepest part of the water, a pool beneath a small waterfall.

I look down at myself; I hadn't even noticed what a mess I am. My clothes are torn and when I take them off there are bruises all over my arms and legs. When I get in the water Hex uses his fingers to gently clean away the dried blood on my head. As soon as he touches me I feel like myself again. I lean against his shoulder in the water and gaze up. Sun sparkles through the leaves and the air smells of berries and flowers. It doesn't seem right to relax when so much is uncertain. But my sore, tingling muscles are beginning to unknot in the water and I let myself close my eyes.

"What happened on that ship?" I ask Hex. "How long were we there?"

"Maybe a day or two? I don't know."

"You didn't recognize me."

He's quiet so I open my eyes and look at him. He's scowling. "What did I do?"

"You were angry at me. You said something about me not taking care of my child properly. Getting high. Like you thought I was your mom."

Hex tosses his head so droplets fling off of the tips of his slick black hair. "I'm sorry."

"You didn't know it was me. It's okay."

"I don't know what's going on. Who is casting these spells or whatever they are. We need to try and find the others."

I nod. "And then we have to find a way to get home," I say.

Hex looks down at me, cocks his head, raises his eyebrows. "I'm not sure it's that simple, Pen."

I decide not to ask him what he means. I just want to find the others and leave. There might be fish and berries and fresh water, but there are too many signs of danger. If burying your own body isn't a bad omen, what is? And besides, how do we know that any of this is real? If our corpses weren't real, then maybe this whole island is a hallucination of some kind.

If I were home, I would never leave the pink house again, even if Giants tried to chase me away. I wonder if the house is there anymore or if Bull went back and wrecked it in his rage. I think about my art prints on the ceiling of my room, Ez's paintings, our books, our vegetable garden. It might all be gone.

After we've bathed we dress in our filthy clothes. I wanted to wash them but they wouldn't have dried in time and we both feel vulnerable enough without having to walk around naked.

We go back to explore the woods a little more, following the stream. The trees form a canopy over our heads and pink and white orchids grow up the trunks and hang from the branches. The ground is bright green with moss and the rocks glimmer, crystalline, in the sunshine. We hear birds; it's unmistakable, and I even think I see a squirrel dart by.

When the air starts to cool we follow the stream back to our camp. As we're collecting wood I hear Hex shout my name and I run to his side.

"*I saw an uncanny thing, which horrifies me to speak of.*
From the first sapling that I tore up, its roots dissevered,
There oozed out, drop by drop, a flow of black blood
Fouling the earth with its stains. My whole frame
*   shook in a palsy*
Of chilly fear, and my veins were ice-bound.'"

"What? What are you . . . ?"

He holds up a branch coated in a sticky dark sub-stance. "It's in *The Aeneid*."

Again.

I back away from what I don't want to believe. "Bleeding wood."

"Yes. It's a sign we should bury someone."

In the book it was because Polydorus, the son of the Trojan king Priam, had been killed and the blood signi-fied that Aeneas must give Polydorus a proper burial.

I turn away, trying to keep the desperation out of my voice, but the thought of the dripping branch makes it difficult. "There's no one else to bury."

"Not yet," Hex says.

I turn back to him. He holds the branch up again but there's no sign of the blood anymore. "Something nasty is going on, isn't it?" After the Earth Shaker, *The Odyssey* had at least provided us with some clues, served as a sort of guide. The parallels with *The Aeneid* are less clear, perhaps a testament to the ever-growing chaos of the world around us.

If stories are no longer our salvation we have even less hope than before.

We build another fire from branches that do not bleed and make our bed on the moss among the roots of a tree. I try to tell Hex that one of us should stay awake, keep watch—what if some other plant decides to hemorrhage in the night—but I'm too tired and sleep is welcome. As a goddess.

8

THE FLOWER CRADLE

THREE CREATURES ARE STANDING over me and Hex.

They are young women with long hair and skin that shimmers wetly in the sunlight. Their breasts, legs, and feet are bare and they wear silk scarves tied around their hips. But they're not ordinary women. Colorful layers of feathers grow from their shoulders and the webbing of wings that are attached on the undersides of their arms. It's like a work by Viktor Vasnetsov, a Russian painter of the late nineteenth and early twentieth centuries. The painting I'm reminded of depicts two women, one fair, one dark, with the bodies and wings and talons of birds. They are perched in a tree, singing siren songs.

"Why have you come here?" the black-haired and feathered creature before me asks.

"Our ship crashed on this island," I say as Hex and I clamber to our feet, using each other for support.

Her golden eyes flash. "You must come with us."

The three of them lift their arms in unison, a flare of color and a shwoosh of wind as their shoulders seem to dislocate and wings fan open; I move closer to Hex.

"We just want to get home," I tell the bird women.

"Home," they say, fixing us with their molten gaze, flapping their gaudy pinions. "Go home."

"We don't know how. We've been trying but our ship is ruined."

"Ruined," they all say.

They are still eying me with great scrutiny and I gulp down saliva.

"You must come with us to see the king."

"Who?" I ask, but I already know. I whisper to Hex, reminding him of my vision of the crowned man but Hex has probably already thought of that.

"The king of the Island of Love." They high step in the sand as if doing some synchronized dance. "He's been waiting for you."

I have to repress a shudder. Hex and I exchange a glance, which tells me he's feeling the same icy signal of warning to his nerve endings. I'm afraid to go but we must meet this king, if he's the same one with Venice, Ez, and Ash in my vision. He was in my dream, too, and in the other vision, the one I had before we left. As was this island. The women call it Love; I told Ez and Ash it was the Island of Excess Love.

"Take us there. Please," I say.

We follow the bird women along the beach, in the opposite direction from the forest and across sand dunes. Spreading out below us on the other side of the dunes is an expanse of green hills covered with citrus groves, grape orchards, and palm trees. A drove of deer are grazing there.

"It looks like we won't have to deal with any Giants at least," Hex says, nodding at the herd.

But what will we have to deal with?

There's a large structure glittering in the distance. As we draw nearer I see that it seems to be made of rough-hewn quartz crystal. Flowering trees and bushes grow in profusion in a large terraced garden in front of the entrance. Bees and blue, yellow, and white butterflies, all as big as my hand, are busy pollinating. I even see some orange butterflies, which were my guide after the Earth Shaker, some kind of sign from my mother leading me to my destination. But I'm not sure I trust these orange butterflies, or any of this for that matter. It could be a mirage to lure us to some new danger.

"What is this place?" I ask.

"The Flower Cradle," the bird women say, in unison.

We pass under a large quartz archway and into a courtyard. More citrus trees grow here—lemon, orange, and lime—as well as fig, apple, pear, and olive trees. Waterfalls splash over rocks into shallow pools surrounded by dark purple roses.

I stop in front of one voluminous blossom that grows eye level with me as if asking me to pick it. I've never seen a rose this color before. Almost like black grapes, that shiny and juicy looking. The perfume it exudes makes me dizzy.

I reach to pluck the flower, without thinking. The stem snaps unevenly and I have to pull hard and at an angle to break the bloom the rest of the way off.

The brown-haired bird woman turns her head sideways, watching me. "Why did you do that?"

"I don't know." I should have picked an orange instead. But the rose compelled me somehow. Like Beauty in the fairy tale.

The red-haired bird woman makes a *tsk*ing sound. I stare down at the rose, wishing I could fasten it back on its stem.

We follow the women through another archway at the far end of the courtyard.

Then we're in a large room of the same rough-hewn quartz with waterfalls cascading down the walls into pools. The floor is polished and inlaid with different-colored stone to create the image of a naked man standing in a circle with his limbs outstretched. He's surrounded by symbols—a sun, a moon, a rose, a dove, a single eye. At the far end of the room is the flower-heaped, incense-smoked dais I saw in my vision. And on the dais is a throne, a huge piece of quartz that's been cloven down the middle to reveal its dazzling innards. Seated on it is the king.

The very young alchemist stared at the people flying off the buildings on the TV screen. For one heart-banging beat he wondered if they had discovered the magic spell to make them fly.

It was not that.

The plane had crashed through the buildings. His mother came in, turned off the TV, and told him to go to his room and get ready for school.

Instead he went to his sister's room; she was seated on the floor, her three black hound dogs sitting upright behind her, her black-, red-, and yellow-striped snake asleep in its cage. Black candles burned and a sketchbook lay open. There was an image on the page of a naked man and woman holding each other in a fountain. The man wore antlers on his head and the woman was missing one eye. Next to it was another image—two skeletons in the same intertwined position with roses growing on and among their bones. A third image was of a young boy with a white dove, surrounded by cryptic symbols.

His sister looked up at him pale-bluely, her eyes so like his that it sometimes confused him.

"Did you see the TV?" he said.

"I felt sick all night," she answered.

He didn't know what this meant. That she'd seen it? That she hadn't because she was sick? That she was sick because she knew what happened before it happened? The last option was not unlikely if you happened to be his sister.

"Can I stay here?" he asked.

She shrugged and he sat down on the floor with her. The curtains were drawn and the room was dim although it was morning. Her hair seemed to be the only source of light.

"This world sucks," he said.

His sister ignored him.

"What are you doing?"

She looked up and stared at him again with her faintly shining eyes. "Witchcraft. Magic. What do you think I'm doing?"

"I want to learn."

"You don't learn, it. You either have the gift or not."

"What are you going to do?"

The three dogs, who had remained almost motionless, began to bay, as if at the full moon of her presence. "I'm going to change the world," she said.

She never did. Not even in the little ways that everyone does, except changing his world when she left it. The gift? He achieved it. But by then it was too late.

I recognize the young man from the twice-reoccurring image in my head, especially the wide-set pale eyes. The only difference is that the crown of antlers he wears doesn't look like a crown. It appears that there are actual antlers growing from his head.

He's like no one I've ever seen. There's something predatory about his high cheekbones, arched eyebrows, and flared nostrils. My heart trembles in spite of itself. I'm usually not this susceptible to beauty, especially male beauty, but there is something about him that makes me feel urgent and unsteady. I glance at Hex but I can't decipher what he's thinking. There is no sign of Venice, Argos, Ez, or Ash.

I try to stay focused on them, but instead all I can think about is the king. I've never been this seized by a vision of someone on our first meeting.

I take a step back from the dais, wanting to make this vision go away. I don't look at Hex but I can feel him watching me and I know his jaw and fists are clenched.

"Where is my brother?" I say, remembering why we are here. "Where are our friends?"

The king keeps staring at me from under his eyebrows. His full lips spread, revealing the dangerous white points of his teeth. "Welcome, my queen" is all he says.

9

THE KING

HEX STEPS FORWARD, seething. "We need to see our friends now."

The king smiles at him but his eyes are serious, sad even. "I'm sorry, Hexane. First you will bathe and dress. You will see your friends at the banquet tonight."

I reach for Hex's arm but he shrugs me off and moves closer to the king. "So you have some tricks? Okay. You speak all fancy and shit, you know my name and you can make us see our dead bodies. You live in a pretty nice place considering the rest of the world has gone to shit as far as I can tell. But that doesn't mean you can dick around with us."

The king's lips curl as if he's smelled something unpleasant. "I don't appreciate that kind of language around my queen."

"What the fuck? And by the way? She's not actually yours. She doesn't belong to anyone. But if she did, homey? It would be me."

"Penelope," the king says. "What do you have to say for this boy?"

"I apologize," I stammer, grasping the back of Hex's shirt and tugging to signal for him to be quiet. "We're both very tired and upset. If we could please just see Venice and Ez and Ash. And our dog, Argos?"

"You will, you will, but first I want you to be presentable. Storm, Dark, and Swift will show you to your chambers." He nods at the bird women; I'd almost forgotten about them. *Storm, Dark, Swift.* Aello, meaning "storm-swift," Celaeno, meaning "the dark," and Ocypete, meaning "swift wing" or "swift-flying," were the names of harpies in mythology. Harpies cursed Aeneas and his men on their way to what would later become Rome. I'm not surprised these women are named after the harpies, although they're much more attractive than the original winged, bird-legged coven.

The king seems to have a large amount of affectations at his fingertips, and on his brow if you count the antlers.

I whisper to Hex, "Please do as he says. I saw every-body here, in the vision." *Venice, Ez, Ash, Argos.* "I think he's telling the truth."

Hex nods but his eyes are hard. Still, he comes with me as we follow the bird women down a corridor.

We stop at a doorway. "Your room," one of our host-esses says to me. Hex starts to enter but she holds him back. "You're next door."

"Fuck that."

I put my hand on his arm. "It's okay. Just for now," I softly tell him. I don't want to cause any trouble. We need to see our friends.

"Whatever," Hex says without glancing back as he's led to his room.

My room has a large bed on a platform of polished quartz. The floor is inlaid with an image of a rose. Inside the rose is an eye.

On a quartz table is a bowl of water, a pile of linens, a vase of the purple-black roses, and a platter of fruit. Dresses hang from protruding crystals of green, black, and pink tourmaline that grow from the quartz walls. The dresses are all of a similar style—long, narrow, cut on the bias, and made of silk or satin charmeuse like the finest slips. Some have tulle at the hem or lace inserts. They are in a variety of colors—ivory, gold, silver, dusky rose, peach, apricot, saffron, sunlit-leaf-green, a celestialous blue. Some, like the blue one, are covered with crystal beading resembling a starry sky. They all look exactly my size although I can't remember the last time I actually wore a dress—maybe my graduation from elementary school, Then? And I hated it. The dry skin of my finger snags on the blue dress and I let go. Standing there, I get the distinct hair-on-the-back-of-the-neck-raising impression that I'm being watched and I turn around.

I'm watching me.

There's a portrait of me on the wall. I hadn't noticed it when I walked in. It's definitely me, but with long hair like I had Then, more sensual lips, a stronger jaw, and two eyes. Three if you count the huge eye on a small platter in my portrait's hand. Bull the Cyclops's eye. The quality of the paint is rich and glossy, infused with light. I'm bare breasted and corpse pale, and there are wilting red roses surrounding me, very much like the ones in the Dante Gabriel Rossetti painting *Venus Verticordia*. In fact the whole painting, down to the butterflies in my hair, resembles the Rossetti. Goose bumps rise up on my arms, in contrast to the smooth skin of the girl in the portrait.

Who is this king and what does he want from us? From me?

I start to call for Hex but stop myself. He'd only get angrier and then we'd be in more danger. It seems wiser to work this strange man's ego to our advantage especially if he's as fascinated with me as he seems.

I try to ignore the warm flush spreading across the tops of my breasts as if my naked body has just been viewed by an enchanting stranger.

Pen, stop. Stay focused.

There's an adjoining bathroom with a sunken quartz tub, a bowl of fresh rose petals on the rim. Running water?

I fill the tub, sprinkle the petals in the water, and step in. I try not to think of anything or anyone as I soap and rinse my body. Then I towel off and put on the blue dress. I fasten my wet hair up on my head and put on a pair of taupe suede boots. There are no underclothes and my own are filthy so I remain uncomfortably naked under the dress, but also soothed by the drape of the fabric on my clean skin. I have to go find Hex. Despite the weird circumstances I'm excited for him to see me bathed and dressed like a pretty girl for once. And what about our host? Do I care what he thinks, too?

Before I leave the room I examine myself in a mirror over the bureau. The ragged patch over my eye ruins the whole effect. I glance down and see a small crystal bowl.

In it is an eye.

An eye so lifelike it could be real.

But it's made of glass.

It's brown, just like mine.

I pick it up and roll it gently between my thumb and forefinger. It feels cool and hard but just slightly malleable, which strikes me as strange.

Without thinking I place it in my empty socket.

Immediately I close my right eye to check—because this can't be.

I can see.

I can see from the glass eye.

The view is blurry like looking through foggy glass but I can see all the same.

I start to cry. Tears fall down my face. From both eyes.

No. I don't want all this. Who is this magician, this sorcerer? Why is he doing this?

I rush out into the corridor and bump into Hex. I gesture to my eye but I can't speak.

"What is it? A glass eye? What's wrong?"

"I can see through it," I say. "Hex, I can see."

He shakes off some invisible shackles. "We have to find Venice, Ez, and Ash and get the hell out of here."

"Okay," I whisper. I can't tell my lover and best friend

that, although I know he's probably right, I feel a pro-
found and confounding need to stay.

"Hexane," the king says when we enter the room where
he still sits, "you didn't put on the clothes I left for you."

Hex shrugs. "I prefer my own, thanks."

"We'll see," the king says.

Hex has met his "we'll see" match. I take a step forward, squaring my shoulders. "Can you explain all this
to us?"

The king smiles and stands. "All what? This place?
What you found in your room? Why question it?"

I try not to flinch and fall to my knees under his blue
agate gaze. Instead we follow him out of the room and into
another corridor. "Because I like to understand," I say.

"Of course you do. And you will."

This isn't enough for me. I force myself to keep talking.
"We were brought here on a ship. We had all kinds of hal-
lucinations, I thought I was going insane, and then there
was a wreck and when we came to on the beach Hex and
I saw two corpses that looked like us and a tree that bled."

"A bleeding tree?" The king frowns and shakes his
head. "That's not how it was intended to go. I'm sorry you
were traumatized and I couldn't explain all of it even if I

chose to. But now it's time for you to regain your strength and see some friends who've been waiting for you."

He ushers us into another room and there they are.

Argos skids across the smooth inlaid floor and I pick him up in my arms, letting him shnuzzle my neck and kiss my face. He's shaking all over with excitement.

Venice, Ez, and Ash sit on cushions at a long low table with a shallow pool of water down the center. Pink lotus flowers grow in the water and koi fish swim there. Six-foot-tall candles light the room and crystals that are almost that tall stand in each corner. My beloved boys are bathed and groomed, wearing linen shirts and trousers, but they could be covered in mud for all I care.

"Pen!" Venice runs to me, followed by Ez and Ash. I bury my face in the nest their shoulders make for me. They smell like olives, honey, and fresh but slightly acrid herbs. My muscles feel as if they're going to collapse with relief.

Venice grabs my arm. "Your eye."

"I'll tell you later," I whisper, not wanting to admit to our host how indebted I already feel to him. He's watching me now, his own eyes as multifaceted as the crystals in the room. "But tell me about you guys," I say louder.

"We woke up here. There must have been a ship-wreck." Ez hugs me again and our sharp clavicles bump. "Ow, you're too skinny."

"You should talk," I say.

"At least I'm eating now, thanks to our host." He gives the king a shy half smile. "And you're going to, too. Look!" He drags me to the table. There are platters of fresh fish, rice, and vegetables wrapped in grape leaves.

My brother is still clinging to my arm. "We were scared you were . . ."

"I know. Same here."

I brush his hair off his forehead. "What about Merk?"

Venice shakes his head, Ash scowls, and Ez says, "We don't know."

Now that I have my boys I'm able to think about my father. I need him, too, I realize. We were all under that spell, not just him. Where is he? But I know I can't ask the king about this now. Not yet.

"Ezra is right. You must eat," he says, still staring at me.

I guess they're pretty close already; Ez never let any-one call him Ezra except his twin brother. Not even Ash calls him that.

On the wall over the table hangs an oil painting of a young woman with blue-ice eyes and white-ice hair crowned with black roses. A white dove is on one shoulder and she's holding a toad in her hand. Though she's upright and her eyes are open, there's a deadness to her face; this and the quality of the paint remind me of John Everett Millais's *Ophelia*. For some reason besides this the woman in the painting looks familiar, but I can't place her. I'm uneasy with her watching me.

"Who's that?" I ask Ez.

"Isn't it amazing? I want to learn to paint like that. He said he'll teach me."

"Who?" I say. But I know already. The king has many talents.

I notice Ash is frowning. Is he jealous of the king? Ez seems oblivious and I still don't know who the subject of the painting is.

But the food is as delicious as it looks and smells, so good that as I eat I forget everything else. For dessert there are figs and tea with honey. The tea tastes of peppermint, chamomile, sage, hickory, and red raspberry, each flavor distinct as if I were eating the fresh herbs. There's also a dark, sweet wine that tastes almost like distilled jewels. We all have some, except for Venice who says it'll make him sleepy and Hex who frowns at me when I take a glass from the king. I take it anyway. My stomach feels satiated for the first time in forever. But I'm afraid of this man who has so much power over us, over the world.

Still, it's hard to resist the pleasure of the moment.

When Argos jumps up and tries to lap from the long pool of water in the middle of the table, the king scoops him in his arms.

"No you don't, little man. You can have some drinking water that doesn't have fish and flowers in it."

"That's why he likes it, though," Venice says.

Argos licks the king by sticking that long dog tongue out of the side of his mouth the way he does with me. Ez gives the king an appreciative glance; he seems just as charmed by him as Argos is. I have a vague memory of telling Ez and Ash a story, describing the king to them before any of this was real.

He sounds dreamy, Ez said.

How much control does this king have over all of us?

Our host puts Argos down; he balances on his hind legs and claps his front paws together. We all laugh, even Ash who is swallowing more wine. But not Hex.

"I'm going to bed," he says when we're done eating.

I lean into him, speaking into his ear. "What's wrong?"

"I don't trust this place, this person. It's all some kind of spell and we need to leave."

"Maybe he can help us find Merk," I say. What I don't say is the king gave us food and baths and beds and clothes and *he gave me my eyesight*.

Hex knows me well; he probably can tell what I'm thinking. He stands and turns away from me, his face shrouded in thoughts. "I'm going to bed," he repeats. "I suggest you and Ez and Ash stop drinking. Your eyes look crazy."

Why would he say that? I remember how he spoke to me on the ship, thinking I was his mother. I know he's sensitive about alcohol since he's sober. The only time he's seen me drunk was at the Lotus Hotel where we met. We both got high on the juice from the lotus flowers. But this is different. This time the wine's being provided by a man with antlers who just gave me back my eye—crazy or not.

"Tell us a bedtime story, Pen!" Ez shouts as Hex leaves the room. He turns to the king. "Pen is a storyteller."

"I've sensed as much," the king says, smiling with so much unexpected warmth that I feel it beaming into me. "I'd love to hear a bedtime story, Penelope."

Ash hands me another glass of wine. "Come on, Pen, show us what you got."

"Yes, please do," says the king.

"We have to convince her that it's a gift," Ez tells him. "She tends to undervalue herself."

"Ezra, I think you're right. That Penelope doesn't see her true worth. She's a remarkable woman."

Now the warmth is overt and I flit my eyes away from his. How can he make me react so strongly with just a word and a glance?

"Go on, Pen," Venice encourages.

So I stare at the painting on the wall for inspiration. Those blue eyes. Just like the king's.

That's who she is! The girl. The sister. She was in my vision, the one I had when I met him.

"I need Ash to sing to help me," I say, hoping to engage him; he's getting really drunk.

Ash shrugs and takes another swallow of wine. His eyes gaze upward at the quartz ceiling as he sings. Even drunk he sounds like an angel.

I start to speak.

I don't mean to upset the king. Maybe it's the wine. Maybe I'm subconsciously trying to distance myself from him. Maybe it's Ash's drunken song. But this is the story I tell.

It was almost exactly a year later on the eve of the event that she had seen coming.

The boy was the one who broke the window of her room with his bare hands. He put his fist through the glass and blood dripped down his wrist like he was the one who had tried to take his life.

She was lying on the floor with her near-albino hair spread out around her and an empty vial of pills by her hand. The three black hounds lay on their sides as if asleep. Even the snake, freed from its cage, did not move when he entered.

His sister's cold blue eyes were open. When he gathered her in his arms her calla-lily skin was cold. Her limbs were stiff. He thought he was supposed to breathe into her mouth but he didn't know how. He opened her mouth. He screamed into it.

She hadn't opened the door for him when he knocked that day and the dogs were missing. He had known something was wrong. He'd tried to call his mother but she didn't answer. That was when he decided to break the window.

When the paramedics came he crouched in a corner, holding one of her books. They tried to take it from him but he wouldn't let them. He rode in the ambulance to the hospital, gripping it to his chest.

His mother met him there. She couldn't walk and they put her in a wheelchair. She kept saying, "No, no, no" over and over. He wanted to scream at her to shut up.

His sister had left a video on her computer. It wasn't for anyone except him. It said, "I'm sorry about Sir, Burr, and Uzi. I needed them on my journey because I kept dreaming of being alone on this road that went on forever. I needed Caduceus, too, although I know you won't miss him that much so I guess I don't have to apologize for that. Snakes rule the afterlife. I really love you, little brother. But this world sucks, you're right. There's nothing I can do from here. Maybe you can.

"Oh yeah. Start by making them cut my hair and bury some smokes with me."

She had taken the dogs and her snake and requested the ciga-rettes; she had left him her books.

He opened the book he had carried to the hospital and brought back again, never letting go. It was filled with drawings of symbols he didn't understand—suns, moons, triangles, hands, serpents, naked figures, doves, toads, angels, dragons, skeletons, swords, eyes. Somewhere in the distance an owl scree-ed like a prophetess of doom, warning of death by poison and death by fire.

Was there a spell, the boy wondered, to bring back the dead?

So he was a regular boy once? If you can call what I saw "regular." He had a sister who killed herself and her three dogs and snake? That doesn't explain much. But my stom-ach contracts and the bones of my chest ache from the vision as if I lived it.

But you didn't. You're you. He's a stranger. Remember this.

The king stands. "Very powerful, my queen," he says. He flicks a speck of dirt, or maybe a tear, off his cheek with his sleeve. "You know many things."

"I'm sorry," I stammer. "I don't know where it came from." The wine is making my head pulse now, the purple blood of grapes engorging my bloodstream, and I need to sleep.

"Storytelling helps determine action," says the king with a prophet's enigmatic smile. "Who knows where this journey will take you. But for now I would like to escort you to your bed."

At the word "bed" my body stirs of its own volition and I clench my thighs together to try to make the sensation stop.

It's afternoon when I wake. As I come back to myself the first thing I do is close my right eye to check. Yes, I can still see out of my left eye.

I go to look for Hex in his room. It's exactly like mine except that it doesn't have the dresses or my portrait. And the pattern on the floor—it's an image of a skeleton standing in a cauldron and holding a sword.

No sign of Hex anywhere.

I go into the dining room, the front room with the throne. No one. I walk outside. Hearing laughter, I cross the courtyard and head under another archway into a grove of fruit trees. Beyond it is a meadow.

Among the wildflowers I see two figures racing each other, followed by a small odd-looking dog, while two other people sit by and watch. The playful gait of the racers makes sense when I realize one of them is Venice but not when I see that the person he's racing has antlers on his head. Aren't those hard to run with? Venice and the king are laughing like little kids and it surprises me; the king didn't strike me as someone who would engage in games with my little brother.

The king calls my name and runs over to me. He's barefoot and bare chested, more muscular than I realized, and his face is flushed. "You slept a long time. Are you rested?"

"Where's Hex?" I demand.

"What? Your friend? He's not in his room? Maybe he went to explore. I'm sure he didn't go far. We've been racing. Your brother is fast."

"Penelope is faster," Venice says, running up, followed by Ez and Ash and Argos. My dog never looked so happy. His tongue is practically touching the ground and his eyes are a-shine. When the king bends down to pat his head Argos jumps up and licks his face, which doesn't seem to bother our host at all.

Ez puts his arms around me and kisses my cheeks. I may never let go of him, Ash, or Venice again.

"So you're faster than your brother?" The king cocks an eyebrow at me. "Care to race and prove it? To that rock and back."

I ignore him and turn to the others. "Have you seen Hex?"

"We checked his room when we woke up," Ez says. "I thought he was with you and we didn't want to interrupt you."

I'm aware of something dark passing beneath the surface brightness of the king's sunlit face.

"I don't get why he was upset last night," Ez goes on. "The food is so good here! Everything's perfect! Right, Ash?"

Ash doesn't answer; he collapses onto a picnic cloth and uncorks a bottle of wine to drink. I wonder if he really is jealous of Ez's relationship with the king. He's never been jealous of anyone before. But we really haven't had any other handsome young men around until now.

"I'll send someone to look for Hexane," the king says. "Now have some food and then let's race."

"See?" says Ez, pulling me over to the picnic. "The food is amazing! We can never leave here." Figs, apples, pears, small cheeses wrapped in fig leaves, a loaf of bread with honey.

We can never leave.

This worries me but it doesn't seem to bother my companions. Even Ash is now gnawing away blissfully at his lunch.

"How come you have all this food?" I ask the king. "Do you know what it's like out there?" I gesture to the horizon, in the direction of the sea that brought us.

"I grow fruits, vegetables, and grains, keep bees, goats, chickens. We fish in the rivers. It's all very simple cuisine but I hope you enjoy it."

"But how? Where is this place?"

"The Flower Cradle. Just a little something I dreamed up. Now eat. I'll go tell one of the girls to look for your friend."

Once again, I'm too hungry to question much. Venice, Ez, Ash, Argos, and I eat our fill and rest on the grass while the king is gone. We don't speak, lulled by the ambrosial smells in the warm air, the blue of the sky full of small white clouds, the sway of flowers against our skin. I pick some blossoms and weave them into Ash's dreadlocks. He seems too drunk to notice. When the king returns, promising he's sent the bird woman Dark to look for Hex, I agree to race him. "But I don't have the right clothes," I say, gesturing to the apricot silk dress I slept in last night.

He flashes his teeth at me. "You look lovely. But if you'd like you can tear off the hem so it's easier to run in. There are lots more dresses."

I ask him how come there are so many and why he's given them to me.

"We have silkworms here, and master weavers. And I told you why. I don't want to upset you but I've known about you for a long time and I know you are my queen."

I realize there's no way to have a logical conversation with him, but then, most things aren't logical anymore.

"I'll style you," Ash says. "Never fear. You won't even remember what Lycra was when I'm done with you." This causes him and Ez to burst into a fit of giggles. I guess the wine eased whatever tension there was between them.

"Are you guys drunk?" I ask, thinking of Hex. *Your eyes look crazy.*

"We're drunk on love," Ez says.

"The Island of Love," says Ash. "Get it? We're drunk, on the Island of Love." He gets down on his knees and rips the hem off the dress so it stops just above my knee with enough extra fabric left to knot between my legs. We use the torn-off fabric to bind my breasts since I still don't have any undergarments. I notice the king watching me as Ash ties the material over my bust and I look down, hoping I'm not blushing too obviously.

I didn't used to be a very fast runner—I was too awkward. Venice was the athlete in the family. But since the Earth Shaker I've gotten stronger from working out with Hex and Venice, in spite of our meager diet.

Where is Hex? I don't like that he hasn't shown up yet; it makes me jittery. Maybe the run will do me good.

"Ready, set, go!" Venice calls out and the king and I take off across the meadow.

The long grasses tickle my shins and the sun shines in my eyes. Eyes! My heart booms blood to my eardrums as I try to keep pace with this man's long legs. He's ahead of me and I don't want him to beat me. I want to show him how strong I am, that he can't win me over so easily with all his praise and trickery. I move my arms quicker, keeping them close to my sides, my head up, shoulders back.

Maybe he lets me, I'm not sure, but I catch up with him as we each touch one of Venice's outstretched hands.

I collapse to the ground, gasping for breath. The king falls down next to me. His chest is heaving, too, and there's a sheen of sweat on his skin. Out of the corner of my eye I can see the smooth indentations of his biceps and pectorals. He rolls over on one elbow and smiles. The disconcerting antlers throw a shadow across my face.

The boy stared down at his sister lying in her pink satin–lined coffin with white lilies all around. Even with her shorn hair she looked like an angel. An angel who had poisoned her three black dogs and killed her snake to keep her company. Her white hands were folded like wings and he managed to slip the pack of cigarettes under them. And then to discreetly snip a lock of her hair and hide it in his pocket. He imagined climbing into the casket with her. It would be dark. They would be there in the dark forever together.

But no, he was going to be strong. He was going to

change things for himself and for his beloved when he finally found her. He was going to learn to use magic and change the world.

"Are you all right?" the king asks.

"I'm fine," I say, not wanting to let him know what I've just seen or how hard the race was, especially if he let me win.

"You have something . . ." He reaches over and brushes a blade of grass off my cheek, cupping my face in his hand, briefly, his eyes on mine.

I don't like how this gesture makes my heart rate accelerate. Aware of my brother and friends watching me I stand up and adjust the torn silk dress.

"And now, for our archery contest," the king announces, jumping to my side. He opens a large leather sack and produces a bow and a quiver of arrows. "The winner will receive this. Venice?"

My brother takes the bow and examines it. "I've never done this before."

"But you have good hand-eye coordination, I'm sure. From all the sports you've done. Just focus, breathe, and pull. Also don't forget the tension in the arm that's not pulling, the bow arm."

"What are we shooting?"

The king points up into the sky. A flock of white doves. Perhaps the same twelve Hex and I saw when we first arrived on the island. They hover just above us as if waiting to be taken down.

"I can't kill them," Venice says.

The king accepts the bow back and addresses Ez and Ash. "I don't suppose you two will shoot at birds either."

They exchange a glance, shrug, and shake their heads no.

The king turns to me. "Pen? They aren't like the birds we once had. They won't die. They only transform."

I squint at him in the crocus-yellow sunlight. "Really?"

"Yes, really. I'll show you." He strings the bow with an arrow from the quiver, aims, and pulls the bowstring. The shaft pierces one bird.

I take in a sharp breath of air, remembering the dove in the dream about my mother.

But when the creature stonefalls to the ground she is no longer a bird but a white rose pierced through by an arrow and still miraculously intact. The other doves, unstartled, reconfigure in the sky just above our heads.

"It would be good for you to have your own weapon to fight off danger," the king says, fitting another arrow into the bow. "That is, if your aim is true, which is debatable." He smiles and runs a hand through his hair. It falls perfectly back into place. I think of yellow petals.

Challenged, I take the bow from him. I've never done this before but for some reason, right now, it doesn't seem that difficult. Still, I don't really want to shoot at a bird when I haven't seen one in so long.

They won't die. They only transform.

Do I believe him? I want to believe him. This is a way to test his veracity. By putting a small, precious life at stake . . .

I point the arrow at a dove. Equal tension in both arms. Remembering what Hex once told me about sword fighting: *When you strike, it is not a thought. It is pure action. You embody the result.*

Keeping my eye on the white bird—*it will fall to earth a rose, Pen*—I pull back the bow and release.

We all stand transfixed as my arrow ascends into the sky and catches fire, blazing into the clouds like a comet until the flame burns out. The birds scatter, unharmed.

"What was that?" Venice asks.

"I have no idea," I say. At least I didn't kill any doves.

"Another sign of your nobility," the king intones. "The bow and quiver are yours, Queen Penelope. May you use them well as you reign at my side."

Reign at his side? The flame of the afternoon's

fantasy sizzles out like my burning arrow. I am no queen. Just a girl without the best aim and an arrow that turned to fire. Although I'm not sure what this means, I know it happened to Acestes, a Sicilian king who provided a brief reprieve for Aeneas and his men before they set off on their journey once more. *The Aeneid* again. Hex's maddening book. Our book. I have to find Hex.

As if on cue, the dark-haired bird woman approaches across the meadow. "The boy is with Swift at the waterfall," she says. She's bare breasted and I notice Venice blush and look away. He hasn't seen any women besides me in a long time, let alone a half-naked one with wings.

The king thanks her and turns to me. "Queen Penelope?"

"Stop calling me that."

"It's just a short ways away. It's a little paradise and we can swim. You can all come. Then we'll be back here for supper."

Ez jumps up, grabs Ash's hand, and dances around with Argos nipping at their ankles.

Even Ash seems happy now, like we're vacationing rather than stranded on an island with a spell-wielding antlered person who seems to have infatuated Ez. We just need Hex to make it okay.

So we agree to go.

The waterfall is across the meadow, beyond an out-cropping of the quartz rock and among a cluster of palm trees. We make our way along the trail toward the sound and smell of water. When we emerge from the trees the air is misty and a waterfall cascades over high rocks into a pool. The king dives in, followed by Ez and then Venice. Dark perches on a rock, watching them, her distracting breasts on display. I turn to Ash.

"What's going on? Do you have any idea?"

He shrugs. "I just want some more of that wine."

I ignore this. "Where do you think Hex is? He wouldn't just leave, would he?"

I'm not so sure. The way he's been acting toward me lately—so cold last night and almost cruel when we were on the boat. Maybe he's still under that spell. But where would he have gone?

"Maybe he's looking for Merk?" Ash suggests. He pulls off his linen shirt and squats on a rock in the sun.

"He would have told me, though."

Ash squints across the water at the king, splashing with Ez and Venice, tiny rainbow droplets flying in the air around them. "Who knows? That guy's up to something. At least he has good wine."

"Come on, Pen, join us!" Ez shouts.

"Where's Hex?" I look over at the one called Dark. "You said your friend brought him here."

"That's what Storm told me." Her eyes are more golden in the sun.

"We'll find him, I promise," the king says. "Come in the water now, Penelope. It's your element. You must become as deeply acquainted with it as possible for when you need it most."

Could he be more cryptic? He seems to be full of these statements. Maybe he knows what happened after the Earth Shaker when that wave came at our house. How would he know this, though, unless he can see things the way I can, which I wouldn't put past him.

But no matter what he means or how he knows what he does, he's right; I may have shot a burning arrow but water is my element. And I need as much fresh water as possible, it seems, to make up for the months without it. We all do.

Venice climbs out of the pool, then jumps off a rock back in, and Ez follows him. Ash closes his eyes as if trying to shut us all out and lies back on the rock to sunbathe.

I remember swimming with Hex, just a day ago. Was it? It seems like forever. Where is he?

But despite the nagging question, I let myself slide into the pool as if putting on a warm silk dress. The actual silk dress I'm wearing provides no significant cover so I try to stay under the water to keep the king from seeing the contours and shadows of my body. He is watching me from a slight distance, smiling. Then he disappears under the water, only the tips of his antlers skimming the surface.

When I'm turned away watching Venice dive I feel hands lifting me up and I scream like the type of girl I never want to be. I can't afford to act silly and weak.

It's the king, holding me by the waist from behind. He grins at me and the predatory look is gone from his face; he's just a playful young man now—well, one with antlers, but still. His muscled arms gleam with water and sunlight. I feel my body giving in, like a plant in need of nourishment.

He owns you, I think. *You are his.*

No, I'm Hex's if anyone's. Where is Hex?

But Hex isn't here and I splash and swim with the king—aware that I'm slipping deeper under the spell of his skin and eyes and smile and not able to fight it, not sure I want to fight it—until the air gets cooler and we decide to hike back.

In my room I change out of the ruined silk dress and into a fresh gown in an ivory color with blush pink lace, and a pair of crimson suede boots that lace up my leg. I fasten a necklace of irregularly shaped rose-tinged baroque pearls around my neck and set a wreath of gold and silver leaves on my head. My stomach rumbles and I put my hand there, feeling the muscles under the thin fabric. I'm still uncomfortable about not having any underclothes. I could ask our host for some but of course I won't give him that satisfaction. He's already proprietary enough.

And you are letting him own you, I chastise myself. *You are wearing his collar.* But I don't remove the pearls.

"Queen Penelope," I say to the woman in the mirror, meaning to sound angry and ironic but it comes out almost proud. Strange. And stranger still is the countenance that looks back at me as if breathed upon by the goddess of beauty herself. I hardly recognize my own reflection.

When I return to the dining room to meet the others for an evening meal the candles are lit, violet twilight glowing through the windows. On the table is more tea and a meal of seafood stew with rice and a salad of fresh greens, berries, nuts, crumbled goat cheese, and nasturtium flowers. And wine. While we eat, the king talks to Ez about painting.

"It's really just creating illusions, isn't it?" the king says. "The illusion of depth, of light, of soul."

Ez is leaning forward, hanging on his words. "But how?"

"You probably know more about that than I do."

"I doubt that. These are masterpieces. Did you get this ability after the Earth Shaker?"

"I guess you could say that, in a way," the king replies.

Ash rolls his eyes and sips more wine. Ez doesn't notice; he's too busy watching the king.

"I'd like to paint you," Ez says.

The king shakes hair from his eyes and smiles. "That could be arranged." He turns to me, hands me a crystal goblet, and I take a sip. This wine is black as blood.

"I'm going to bed," Ash says coolly. Ez hardly notices him leave.

The sun and water of the day has made me drowsy. Soon I'm reclining against pillows with my friend and my brother and my host, forgetting, I'm ashamed to say, my lover. Perhaps Ez has forgotten his lover a little, too.

Hex isn't in his bedroom when I stumble there, tracing my fingers along the quartz wall. I go to my room, fall to the bed fully clothed and sleep.

Later, I feel sweet-warm breath on my face—the exhale of jasmine flowers on a spring breeze, and open my eyes, reaching out in the darkness for Hex.

But it's not Hex.

The king sits on my bed, his antlers branching out into the darkness and entwined with pink-white jasmine blossoms, olive branches, and grape leaves. He's holding a large crystal goblet in one hand and a candelabra in the other. The candlelight throws shadows across his face and ignites his eyes and the gold hoops in his ears. I sit up and cover my chest with the bedsheets. I'm wearing the cream silk charmeuse gown and my hair is slicked back with oil that smells like lily of the valley. I reach to make sure my new eye is still there. It is.

"Don't be scared," he says. I can feel my body melting like dripping wax with the heat of his voice.

"Why are you here?" I ask.

"I brought you some wine to help you sleep."

"I *was* asleep." I try to sound angry but it's hard with him this close. I smell dark roses, grapes, and honey.

"I'm sorry." His eyes twinkle in the light of his smile. "Well, since you are awake now anyway, would you like a libation?"

"Libation? Isn't that ceremonial?" The liquid shines darkly in the crystal goblet. I'm suddenly very thirsty. I take the cup in both hands, lower my lips, and sip.

"Ceremonial? Yes, an offering of sorts. To Sylvan."

"Who?"

"You will know someday."

I have no chance to ponder this name. The wine hits me right away, streaming through my blood and weakening my joints. I blink at the king. He's standing up now, wearing a white linen shirt with shell buttons and brown leather trousers that hang low on his hips and loosely around his thighs. His feet are bare.

"Penelope, I'd like to show you something. Will you come with me?"

He takes the goblet of wine, sets it down, and holds out his hand. It's large and smooth, and he has a gold ring on his middle finger. His nails are carefully shaped, flat, and clean. I guess I was so entranced with his face that I never noticed his hands before.

"Is it Hex? Have you found him?"

"I'm sorry, no. It's something else."

I find myself getting up anyway, taking his hand, walking barefoot over the chilly polished quartz floor depicting that disturbing image of an eye inside a rose. The king lets go of my hand, takes a gold brocade robe that's hanging on some protruding crystals, and places it over my shoulders. He catches my hand in his again. I can feel our pulses mixing where the crook between my thumb and first finger presses into his. I'm not cold now.

His voice is husky. "Come with me."

We climb up the winding staircase into the tower. Tourmaline crystals that protrude from the walls have been fitted with candles lighting our way. At the top of the tower is a large balcony overlooking a garden. I don't remember seeing it before. Trees with silvery bark and others with draping, feathery leaves overhang pools of water that shine in the moonlight. Silver-white orchids grow everywhere and even from here their scent is so strong it's almost like a drug. They're the shape of the *Calypso bulbosa* orchid whose name is from the Greek word for concealment because they tend to grow in hidden areas of forests.

"Watch," the king says, pointing at the flowers.

Dewdrops wink on the petals. That must be what accounts for the silver color, I think. As I watch, some of the blossoms lift off their stems and float around in the air. Insects? I can hear a very high, tinkling music.

"Do you like them?" he asks.

"What are they?"

In answer he holds out his hand and one of the flowers flies toward us and lights on his fingers. Up close I can see that it's not a flower at all but a humanoid creature dressed in petals.

"I thought you should have something like this," the king says.

The winged creature flutters into the air near my

face, pointing its toes and flapping its wings. Its eyes, the glitter I mistook for dewdrops, are on delicate stalks poking out of its head and it has very sharp tiny teeth.

"It will help us learn more about each other."

"What does that mean? I thought you already knew all about me."

He holds out his hand and the wing-thing alights there again. "Yes, and you seem to know a great deal about me as well. I recall you recounting a tale of a boy and his sister."

So that was real, the vision I had? He was the boy in the vision. His sister died. That explains only some of the strangeness. I consider asking him to explain but he speaks again, nodding to the tiny humanoid flower perched on his hand.

"When it touches me you'll be able to see even more into my past and vice versa. Eventually, you may be able to see into the future as well."

I don't tell him that I'm afraid to see more of his past, let alone the future, especially if my other visions were correct. But it's too late. When I look into his eyes again I see . . .

He lived on an island off the California coast, in a small cottage on the grounds of a botanical garden. The walls were painted with the symbols from his sister's book. Large pieces of quartz everywhere, birds in cages, hanging plants, and on the stove a large cauldron filled with purified water and flowers and semi-precious stones. He hoped to cast spells with these things but so far nothing had worked. When he wasn't caring for the plants in the garden he cleaned falcons whose feathers were coated in slick black ooze from an oil spill, helped pelicans whose eggshells had been thinned by exposure to poisons incubate their eggs, rescued fox kits from the talons of golden eagles and ancient, precious plants from marauding wild sheep and pigs.

He had been sitting cross-legged on the floor, high on psychotropic plants, meditating on the fate of his beloved flora and fauna, when the Earth Shaker struck. Everything flew and fell apart around him but he was not afraid. He could envision the destruction of the world and he could envision its rebirth. He knew he was changing and that anything was possible. He would receive a mysterious gift to make everything appear as he wished it. The world would be fresh and free and clean and safe. The world would belong to him and his queen.

The vision fades and I shake myself back to reality, if you can call it that. The startled orchid creature takes off and lands on the king's outstretched hand. Except for the antlers he looks just like he did in the vision. I might have seen glimpses of his past but it's all still a mystery. Who is he? What happened to him?

He's speaking softly like he's in a trance. "You live in a three-story house, painted a pinkish color. There's art everywhere and old books. You had a mother once, very lovely, and a father. Wait . . . I see two men. There was some kind of betrayal.

"You've been through a lot. There is someone I'd have liked to kill for you, but you already did that for yourself. You think you have found the love that you need but there's been something missing. I want to show you what's been missing."

"How are you doing this?" I ask him.

He frowns. "Doing what?"

"All of this."

"There's no need to question anything on the Island of Love. It just is. Enjoy it."

There's a maelstrom in my belly. "It's not just what you know. It's this world you have here. The castle, the paintings, the food. I need more of an explanation than that."

The king studies me for a moment before speaking. "I've been studying magic and alchemy for a long time. When the disaster struck my powers seemed to be awakened. You may know something about this phenomenon?"

Yes. My "powers," if you can call them that, and those of my friends, manifested after the Earth Shaker. That still doesn't explain everything.

"But why?" I ask. "Why did you give me the eye and the dresses and now this?" I gesture to the creature on his hand and its lips part in what might be called a smile. But a weird smile, as if a flower had a mouth. And teeth.

He tugs at a lock of his gold hair. "Don't you like it?"

"That's not the point. You're messing with my head. And I still don't know the reason."

"You're my queen. I told you."

"No," I say. I fold my arms on my chest, trying to will him to explain.

He sighs. "When I was very young my sister, Xandra, drew an image of us. I meditated on that image and I began to see you in my mind. I saw you alone in a room, reading, always reading, looking at paintings, studying the world around you. Your vision was so precious to you; I saw that. Someone who perceives, understands, and values beauty the way you do should never be robbed of even a shadow of her sight."

These words awaken a small sob in my chest. He goes on. "I felt your loneliness as a girl, the unrequited love for your best friend. You were so beautiful to me, so vulnerable, and, though you didn't know it yet, so strong and I knew you must be mine. I have looked for you ever since.

When I found you—in my mind at first—I sent the ship to bring you here, although I didn't cast any evil spells on the ship or make you see your own corpse, as you say." This last thought makes him shudder almost imperceptibly.

"Then who did?"

"I'm not sure. But my intentions toward you are only the most loving kind. You've suffered enough and now I want you to be happy."

"I appreciate everything but I just want to get back home."

The king reaches out to touch my face very gently, then drops his hand, and I find myself wishing he hadn't. "This is your home now."

"What about Hex?"

His brow wrinkles with concern. "I'm sorry. I don't know where he is. He may have left. It happens sometimes. As you've expressed yourself, this place is a lot to take in."

"He wouldn't have left me." Why does my voice sound so uncertain?

"Let's get you back to bed. I just wanted you to see my special orchids."

We lean over the balcony and I look at the flowers again. *I'm glad you woke me. Thank you.*

As I follow the king down the stairs of the tower to my room I realize I don't want to be leaving yet.

He leads me to the door of my room. He takes my hand, and kisses it. I can feel the shape of his lips even after he has left.

In my room, on my bed, is a piece of parchment with words written on it.

dear pen
i had to leave. it doesn't feel safe here. i can tell you are happy not to have to worry about food or water or monsters in the night. and grateful to have your sight. but i need to live in the real world. i know we will meet again. hug ez, ash, ven, and argos for me.
i love you
hex

I stare at the piece of parchment in my hand. It's Hex's writing. The way he signs his name. But I can't believe Hex would write this. As if I mean nothing to him. As if we did not survive the end of the world together. I gasp for air and my legs crumple under me like they are made of the same silk as my dress. As I fall I knock over the goblet of wine the king brought earlier. The crystal shatters and the wine stains the floor. But it's no longer wine. It's too dark, too tinged with the scent of copper. It's blood.

I want to scream out for Ez and Ash, and Venice, who are asleep in their two respective rooms, but I can't pronounce words. Instead a long wail escapes from my throat. In seconds the king is back in the room. He's on the floor with me, his arms around my shoulders. My heart's pounding so hard it's making my bones shake.

"What's wrong? Penelope?"

I show him the note. I don't mean to. I don't even trust him. But I show him the note. It feels at that moment like he's all I have in the world.

"He did leave. Damn."

"He wouldn't leave me," I say. "We're never apart. He's my best friend. He's . . ."

"Come with me. We'll get you something to drink and then you'll rest."

I let him half lift me to my feet and lead me down the hallway to a large room. The walls are all jagged with silvery crystals. The bed is twice the size of the one in my room. In front of it hangs a painting. It's of a bare-chested man with longish gold hair and fair skin. His chest and abdomen are like flat slabs of carved stone. His eyes are fierce blue. Beside him is a creature with a woman's face and breasts but the body of a lion. She's stretched out, long and rippling, eyes closed, leaning her cheekbone against his. It resembles *The Caress*, a painting of a man and his feline muse, by a Belgian artist, Fernand Khnopff. But in this painting the man is the king, without his antlers, and the sphinx is me.

I'm not weak anymore. Adrenaline pounds through my limbs as I face him. I could have a lion's loins with all this force I feel. "What is this?"

"Penelope. I'm sorry it's frightening to you. What we don't understand can be terrifying. But it's better than the real world, believe me. I just want you to be happy."

"Happy? I don't know who you are or what you're doing but there's only been bad magic around me since . . ." I hesitate. Since the first time I dreamed of the king.

"Only bad magic?" He frowns under the shadows of his antlers so lines crease his smooth brow.

"I thought my brother was burning to death. I was forced from my home by Giants. I was taken across the sea on a possessed ship. We almost died! And then we arrived here and Hex and I had to bury ourselves."

The king asks me to slow down and tell him the whole story, from the beginning. When I'm done he picks up what appears to be a single silvery orchid. It's one of the winged creatures, its feet tucked under it, its dewdrop eyes closed. He hands it to me but I shake my head, no, and look away. Still, he's made a point. This is not magic that I can call bad in any way.

"I told you, Penelope, I don't know about these things

you speak of," he says. "I only bewitched you to see beauty. To *hide* the horrors."

I know he is a trickster and a sorcerer but I believe him when he says this.

"But how did you do it?"

"After what you call the Earth Shaker hit, the island where I lived and almost everyone on it was destroyed. Only myself, Storm, Dark, and Swift survived. They had different names then. I was given a gift that allowed me to make what was hideous around me appear beautiful. I made quartz palaces and flower gardens and orchards and waterfalls. I made Storm, Dark, and Swift into demi-goddesses with wings. I did all this with you in mind, the young woman from my visions, knowing one day I could share this world with you. It may be illusory but it is meant only to give you pleasure and solace."

Once again, none of this makes sense but I'm used to that by now. I've accepted that after the Earth Shaker hit, the king was bestowed with strange gifts like the ones my friends and I received. What I really don't understand is why this magician king would care about me at all.

"I'm not a mythical creature. I'm nothing special."

His lips are so full that they turn down even when he's smiling. Now he's not smiling. *The fold of his lip between your lips. No . . .*

"Why would you say that about yourself? After you've

survived what you have, conquered monsters, saved your loved ones. There's enough horror in the world. You don't have to attack yourself, too."

"Leave me alone!" I push at his chest—it's so solid—and he catches my wrists.

"You need to leave yourself alone. Your true self. Stop fighting who you are, Penelope."

His grasp is too strong for me to get away. "Where's Hex? What did you do with him?"

"Penelope, I didn't do anything to Hex. But I want to help you any way I can."

The skin of my belly pulls taut in spite of myself. A sob catches in my throat. I close my eyes, dizzy. The wine I drank earlier . . . I must have had more than I realized.

"Bring him back? Can you bring him back?" Now I'm pleading. I have no other choice.

"I'm sorry. That's one of the things I can't do for you. Not if he doesn't want it. But I can do almost anything else you want."

"What does that mean?" I ask, wary, but wanting.

He gestures around the room. The rough walls split to expose glittering crystals, the smaller, colored crystals growing along the surface, the polished quartz floor with an image of a sun and moon on it, the painting of me as a mythical being and him as a man. Beyond this room is a whole castle of quartz and beyond that are gardens and orchards and meadows and lakes and waterfalls and forests. Untainted, unpoisoned. All this is his and he is offering it to me and my brother and my friends. He offered it to Hex, too, but Hex left. We could have all lived here together. Maybe I still can live here. I don't want to fight any more monsters or grieve the loss of any more loved ones or face each day not sure if I'll survive. But Hex . . .

The king wraps his arms around me, careful not to graze me with his antlers. He's so warm. That scent of roses, grapes, and honey. Also sage and mint. His hair is soft against my cheek but the gold stubble on his chin is rough, scratching, comforting in its own hard way. The muscles of his arms shift and pulse beneath his linen shirt. I bury my face beneath his collarbone. I'm so tired. I don't want to fight anymore. I want all the nightmares to just end. I want to be taken away beyond the pain. That's what I want.

He reclines my body onto the purple silken bedding beneath a canopy bordered with acanthus flowers. I'm passive, a doll; it feels like relief to give in. The silk dress clings to my nipples, breasts, and abdomen, the fabric dipping slightly at the place where my thighs meet my torso. I'm wet there with no underclothes to absorb the moisture. My breath is coming faster and my chest is heaving. The king puts his hand over my heart.

"My queen, how I desire you."

"Always so formal," I whisper, smiling to myself at his affectations.

"I've cultivated the speech that befits a queen. May I lie with you, Penelope?"

"In what sense?" I manage. I guess I mean it as a joke but neither of us laughs.

His eyes refract the light like the crystals out of which his home is made. "In any way you choose."

I shake my head on the pillow, the strands of my hair covering my face, and he gently brushes them away.

"What's wrong?"

I don't want to tell him that I want him too. I have never wanted a man before. It's a sharp ache that feels like it belongs to someone else, yet it's mine. "Am I under a spell?"

"I have been known to cast spells," he says. "But I think you are too strong for me. I think this desire is beyond my magic. It seems to be almost the source of my magic, not the other way around. Do you understand?"

I shake my head, no. I don't understand anything about him.

He is so close now that his breath stirs my hair and he's breathing harder now. "Think of an artist and his muse," he says, moving his hand down to my solar plexus. I feel my heart beat even there. "The muse may look at the painting he makes of her and think, *This is magic!*" His hand moving toward my silk-covered belly. "But the artist created that magic because of her. So the spell belonged to her all along."

Like the painting on the wall of the man and the sphinx. The muse dreaming the artist. Not the other way around. So strange. And stranger still, this desire I feel for the antlered king.

No, I've never been with a man before. I had a crush on a ginger-haired girl named Moira but she liked boys. I fell in love with Hex, thinking he was born male, and loved him the same, or maybe in some ways more, when I discovered he was not. That's the extent of my experience. Hex and I have done a lot sexually and it's always felt safe and right. But Hex is gone now. He left me, with only a note.

The king has bewitched us all, I'm pretty sure. But the world he's made is a paradise of sorts. And it's as if he made it just for me.

I realize that I never answered his earlier question.

"Yes," I whisper.

"Yes, what?"

"You may lie with me."

"In what sense?"

I blink up at his face with its smooth, symmetrical bones. The candle flames flare behind him.

"In any way you choose."

The king moves his hand back up from my belly, over my sternum to my throat. He clasps my neck like his fingers are a gentle piece of jewelry and leans forward so our lips touch, sending a scattering of pearls from my mouth to my groin. As we kiss harder I grasp his hair, tugging gently. My hands move higher up and meet the hard shape of his antlers. Instead of making me retreat, the feel of them excites me more. He silences my moan with more kisses and slips the straps of my dress off my shoulders with one hand, fondling my face with the other one. One hand on my cheek, one hand on my right breast. The nipple rises to his touch and he rubs it gently. His hand moves to the other breast and I grip my thighs together, not as a barricade but as a form of pleading. Who is this creature I've become? It's as if he's transformed me into a sphinx. Should I check to see if I have a spotted hide, sleek-muscled haunches, a tail and claws? The king's still sitting up and I grasp his shoulders and bring him down beside me. He takes one of my hands and moves it over his flat belly to his pelvis while his lips find my breast. Inside me the pearls cascade as I let my fingers move over his hardness, so foreign it might as well belong to another animal. I run my fingers up and down this shaft, feeling it grow even harder. I want him inside me. I need him. This is the most powerful spell of all.

The king shifts his weight, sliding his hand back over my belly and between my thighs, dragging my dress with his wrist until he slips it off over my hips, legs, and feet.

I'm so warm and sleek that I hardly feel naked. Maybe we really are becoming animals. No shame.

But I should feel shame. I'm betraying the one I love.

No, Pen, you are here with me. You are mine. We are all that exists now. I love you.

The voice seems like mine, in my head, but it's his voice, the king's. He's already inside of me, in one way at least.

I'm a naked shameless animal and he's still dressed in his linen clothes. He moves his hand between my legs and pushes my thighs gently apart, skimming my hair with his fingers, dipping lightly inside. I jolt up and he reaches for me, soothes me, lays me down again on the endlessly soft bedding. His mouth continues to plunder mine, drawing out cries of joy I'm unable to stifle.

"Please," I say. "I want you."

"Penelope, are you sure? I don't want this to be imposed on you. I want you to know your own great power."

I gaze into his eyes, which are filled with the reflection of candle flames like lakes surrounded by torches. "I don't care if I'm bewitched. I just want you. Please."

With one hand still between my legs he unfastens the first button of his shirt. I reach up and help him, slipping the shells through the holes, sliding the fabric off his warm, satiny shoulders. His bare chest glows like phosphorus in the dark. I press my lips to his skin, tasting salt and olives, lavender and honey. I reach for the waistband of his trousers and tug to release him. The shock of that smooth skin on that hard shaft makes me gasp for air and he lifts my mouth back up to his and revives me with his kiss.

Somehow he's undressed all the way now, and poised on top of me, pressing my legs apart with the bone width of his knees. One hand rests lightly at my sensitive spot, two fingers rubbing in circles.

"I'll make sure it doesn't hurt," he tells me.

I glance down and understand why he's said this but I'm so excited and open that I'm not afraid. This desire is like a sphinx growling with my throat, thrusting with my pelvis, filling my head with riddles.

Why are you here? Why are you doing this? What have you become? Who are you, Pen? Penelope? Who are you?

Does it matter?

I come a thousand times, a thousand ways, it seems, in the arms of the king.

But once, when I glance up past the marble-pale curve of his deltoid muscle, I think I see three pairs of golden eyes watching us from the dark. I am too drunk with pleasure to pay much attention.

"Dylan, come with us," the girl calls. She has long red hair, a little frayed by the sun. She's running down a beach, wearing a

bikini. Two other girls are with her. One brunette, one with black hair. All gorgeous as nymphs.

The young man they're calling is sitting alone on a rock, looking out at the water. His sun-bleached hair falling ragged over his eyes. He blinks in the direction of the girls and then turns back to the horizon.

The three form a quick circle, speak, giggle, turn and run back to him.

They climb up the rocks, using their outstretched arms for balance. They sit beside him.

"What are you doing?" the black-haired one asks.

"I'm thinking about the future," he says.

"Am I in it?" She speaks with the courage of a girl who knows boys find her beautiful.

He looks at her. His eyes are as blue as the part of the waves where the sun shines directly. But they're cold.

You and your friends will be my winged demi-goddesses, my servants, handmaidens to my beloved when I find her, *he thinks.*

"Not in this form," he says to the girl.

10

ABOMINATIONS

I WAKE TO SCREAMS. Have you ever heard anyone being tortured? Have you ever heard anyone burning to death? There aren't words for this sound. It has to be a nightmare. But it's not; I don't think so.

The room I fell asleep in is gone. I'm dressed in rags fastened together with thorns, lying on a large stone surrounded by weeds and rubble. Here and there I recognize a broken piece of a chair, a smashed cup, some shards of mirror. The air smells not like flowers and honey but like toxic smoke. There is no roof and the sky above me is dark and roiling with clouds.

I slide off the stone, scraping my bare legs.

I run over the ground, cutting my feet on sharp rocks. I run toward the screams. Agonized shrieks. Starting to diminish.

There's a fire burning. Black smoke billows up. The smell of charred flesh meets my nostrils. On the pyre I can make out what looks like a man's body with blackened skin. Then the flames flare up and consume him. On the ground by the fire is a pair of antlers.

In *The Aeneid* the queen, Dido, burned herself on a pyre when her lover Aeneas left her to build a new civilization. But I did not leave the king. Someone took him away from me, took his life.

I reach to touch my left eye socket. There's a piece of glass there, that's all. I shut my right eye to test it out and the world goes black. The magic is gone. The king is dead.

I put one hand to my belly and one to my throat. Other hands catch me from falling. Venice, Ez, Ash, all dressed in rags like me. Argos is with them, too.

"What happened?" Venice says, biting his lip, fighting tears as he stares into the fire. I draw him to me so he can't see. I must protect him; I can't fall apart now.

"I don't know. We have to leave, though."

It's hard to know where to go. The entire landscape has changed. It's just dirt and rubble and rock as far as the eye can see. But the ocean—that's still there. You can smell it on the cold wind. That's where we have to go.

We move as quickly as we can over the ground on our bare feet, trying to avoid broken glass and the sharper rocks.

In my mind I am calling for Hex, even though it's too late, even though he can't hear me. Even though I've betrayed him.

We're down at the beach now. The sand is littered with bones and glass and bricks and splintered wood. But we're by the sea at least. Maybe we can get away. How can we get away?

A body lies broken on the ground. Arms and legs twisted in the wrong directions. Neck risted to the side. Hair and beard matted with blood. Nose cut off, one ear missing. Eyes? Eye sockets. Empty. Birded and beaked.

My mind is made of one-word shrieks of shock.

Merk. Merk. Merk.

My mother is dead, the father who raised me as his own is dead. Much of the world is dead. I held my true love's body and my own body in my arms. I buried us. I blinded a Giant, killed a man. I saw a man I had made love to, just hours before, burned to death. This death before me should be another horror to face and lock away in my mind. But it's not that simple. I've been torn asunder. Merk, my father, my sometime savior and protector, seemed invincible. Even when he disappeared, I was pretty sure he would turn up when we needed him most. But he's not turning up anywhere. Someone or something killed him and pecked out his eyes.

Maybe this is an illusion. Remember your corpse and Hex's. Maybe this is a sinister spell like that was?

But I don't really believe that my father's corpse is an illusion.

Then I smell something—a sulfur stench, like wet rot and decaying corpses and raw sewage—and it feels like it's permeating every single one of my pores. I cover my nose and mouth and struggle to breathe.

Through my watering eye I see them—three haggard old women. Their skin is so dry it's sloughing off in scales and they wear bird skulls around their necks, capes made of dirty feathers trailing over their bare shoulders and wrinkled breasts. Each of them holds a crude spear in one hand.

"You made us do it," they screech. Their teeth look rotten; some are missing.

"Do what?"

"Ruined," they all say.

The largest one goes on. "We were ruined. Once we were young and beautiful like you. Once we would have made almost any boy swoon. But not the king, not him. Even then he was saving himself for you."

"What happened to you?" I ask them.

One takes a step forward on her long scaly legs. Her nails are sharp enough to claw out an eye.

She's close enough now that I can see the raw red patches on her skin. Her eyes are a sickly yellow color. "We are going to die this way. But you, you'll find a way to escape and have a family and a life."

"Unless you don't," the others caw.

I see three girls in bikinis running across the glinting black sand. Their long wet hair—brown, black, red—streams down their sunned backs, almost to their hips. Their nails are painted different pastel colors, the polish chipping off in places; there are strings and strands of shells and beads knotted around their ankles and wrists. They are laughing so hard they're doubling over as they run. All they want is to grow up and meet a handsome, kind man and get a good job and have a kid or two and stay best friends forever. They want to remain on this island with its tall trees and wildflowers and foxes and squirrels and deer and live in little houses. Maybe they all can be next-door neighbors—that would be perfect—and raise their children here and when they die, which is something they don't think about, really, but if they did, they would imagine having their ashes scattered on this sea. This blue sea full of bright fish.

But none of this will come true, except the part about staying together on the island. There are no husbands for them, or babies.

The Earth Shaker has struck this island, followed by the waves. A power plant has been destroyed, spilling its toxic waste, poisoning the few people who remain. Their once brown, green, and blue eyes are round and yellow now, their once smooth legs are scaled, their pretty nails are talons, their taut bellies swollen; over their shoulders are capes made of dirty feathers, useless wings that cannot take them away from this place. Until the king with his whims and spells transforms it into paradise and them into the mythical, winged creatures Storm, Dark, and Swift.

The girls, the way they were, are a lot like three other girls. Like me and my two best friends from Then, Moira and Noey. Moira was a red-haired cheerleader; Noey was a drummer and a photographer with dimples. I was the nerd of the bunch, obsessed with images and words. We were just three girls who loved each other and wanted to be loved and suffered a curse when the world came to an end. If another kind of curse befell us we'd be harpies defecating on ourselves. Instead, two of us are dead and one of us might as well be.

I imagine myself and Moira and Noey as these creatures, here on this island, turned into monsters, shitting ourselves and our food, abandoned, reviled, unable to procreate. I think of the Giants and of the sirens coated in mud in the swamplands back home and the witches and all the stinking, miserable life that is left on this ruined planet. I think of my dead parents and my other father, crazy Merk, my savior, with his eyes pecked out.

And then I think of the king burning to death, the king who wanted to give me a world of wonders, even if it was as illusory as his love for someone with my name and face, someone whom he never really knew. But still . . .

"What did you do?" I rasp.

In answer, they start to hum, an infernal sound.

But Venice is shouting my name. I turn and see a small boat in the water. It's roughly constructed but it seems sound, bobbing there, with two sets of oars. There's a figure in the boat and he's calling our names, beckoning us to come to him.

Hex.

"Burnt offering," one of the harpies says. "The king betrayed us. You are our queen. You can make us what we once were."

"Pen!" Hex shouts. Ez, Ash, and Venice with Argos are running toward him.

"If you leave us here you will face famine, fire, and flood. Your hunger will gnaw at you until you eat the furniture and when that is not enough you will eat each other."

I turn my back on the harpies and head to the boat.

But something sharp strikes me in the right shoulder. I stumble and fall to the sand. My arm explodes. I can't even scream.

Venice pulls me up. Pain like a volcano. Something whizzes past my ear. A spear lands quivering in the sand beside me and my brother. A spear. Like the one that's lodged in my shoulder. Bleeding me out. And this second one could have injured Venice.

There is no room for compassion. These creatures may have once been girls like me and my friends but now they are something else entirely.

With my good left arm I reach for the spear in the sand. Blood like lava is spurting, running down my neck and torso.

I don't have the king's bow and arrow but I have the memory of my spear aflame in the sky. I gather all the power left in my body and focus it into my left hand. Then I trap the image of the largest harpy in the crosshairs of my eye and fling the spear across the sand. It skewers the harpy's breast.

I've killed before, from an even nearer distance. I've felt a knife pierce skin, flesh, and organs. It changed me.

It destroyed me in some way, the me I was before. A deep vicissitude has been required of me. And now I'm changing again. To what I must become.

A third spear is launched toward us. Venice knocks me out of the way. He grabs the spear, puts his arm around me, and pulls me along toward the boat. But I'm too heavy for him and he stumbles.

Now, now, now, Hex is here. He lifts me into his arms and runs. I feel like a child in his arms. So weak. We're almost at the boat. I look back at Venice. He flings the third spear toward the harpies and the second one *shree*s and drops to the ground.

The third harpy, now spearless, is running toward us. "May you be tormented by wars and suffer the loss of your friends. May the blue-eyed child in your belly be served to you as supper. May your corpse go unburied and no one there to witness the bleeding sapling."

"Damn," Hex mutters. "That's some hard-core shit. Way to come up with it on the fly."

All I can think of are the words "the blue-eyed child in your belly." What does this mean? And, "be served to you as supper."

We reach the boat. Ez and Ash help us and I am placed carefully down in the hull.

"Take it out!" I scream at Hex. The force of my voice sends more eruptions of pain through my arm.

The boat is starting to move, away from the island, away from my father's unburied corpse. From my fetal position on the deck I see Ez and Ash at the oars. Venice and Hex are down beside me. Argos is licking my face in methodical strokes.

Hex tentatively touches the spear lodged in my shoulder but he's not doing anything. He's not doing . . . His face looks so white it's as if he's the one who lost all the blood.

"Pull it out and kill her with it!" I say between clenched teeth. "Don't fucking miss!"

"Hold her down," Hex tells Ez.

I brace myself, teeth biting into my lip until I taste the iron tang of blood.

Venice holds me down and Hex pulls. In one executioning blast the spear dislodges from my shoulder with a rip-wrench-crack. The pain is too much, it's too much.

Burnt offering.

The king is dead.

The world is black.

The world is red.

11

THE ISLAND OF
THE SHADES

WE CAN'T STOP THERE," Ez says. "We have to
get back."

"We have no choice," Hex shouts. "We need to get
her on land. She's losing blood. There might be someone
who can help us there."

"Or rip our hearts out and eat them for supper," says
Ash. "I'm kind of over trusting any of these freaks we
keep meeting."

"That girl wouldn't just be sitting there if it was that
dangerous." Now it's Venice speaking.

"If she's even a little girl at all."

What girl? I can't tell if I'm dreaming. I try to sit up
but the pain in my arm knocks me back down.

"We've dealt with worse." Hex puts his hand on my forehead. "She's burning up. We have to stop."

Yes, stop.

I want it all to stop. Once there was a castle made of quartz and a magician king with a stag's crown. Once there was a fire that burned him to ashes like the pyre on which an epic queen took her life. (But the king did not choose his death.) Once there was a killing woman who betrayed her beloved for an enchantment. Her king died; her lover survived. She does not deserve to live.

"I'm sorry," I say.

Hex leans closer. "What, Pen?"

"I'm sorry. I . . . it must have scared you to see us drinking and then you left and he . . ."

A shadow crosses Hex's face. "You don't really know me that well," he says, like we've been having a pleasant chat over lunch but something tasted just a little off. "And I'm not sure how well I know you anymore."

The boat bumps up against some rocks, jolting my arm again. I gasp as Venice—whispering in my ear not to speak, to save my strength—lifts me up so I can see.

The sun is setting, turning the sea to blood. We've reached land, what appears to be a small, rocky island with some very young trees and a smattering of wild-flowers and shrubs. It's not the Island of Excess Love. It's somewhere else. The girl sits perched on an outcropping of bone-colored rock, staring out to sea. Her dark hair has made a cloak for her body. She's maybe ten years old. Even from this far away and in my altered state I can see her green eyes like beacons. I'm relieved we've stopped here, not only for selfish reasons; I can feel that she needs our help, too.

"Ready?" Hex and Venice carry me, with Argos following. Ez and Ash moor the boat on the rocks and come behind us.

The girl doesn't flinch as we approach her. The air is cold and gray and I can taste salt in it. I'm shivering so hard I feel it reverberating in Hex's body.

"We aren't going to hurt you," Venice says. "We need to help my sister."

The girl stands, still wrapped in her thick hair. She and Venice lock eyes as if no one else is here.

"Are you all right?" Venice asks.

She doesn't answer. She just starts to sing in a low, keening whisper.

"Can you help us find water and shelter? Maybe food?" Ez asks. "Please. She's losing blood."

When he says the word "water" I realize that my throat is parched and my tongue swollen as if I haven't had a drink for days. Maybe I haven't.

The girl releases her hair so it whips out around her,

revealing a frail frame dressed in rags and skin the color of nutmeg.

The earth is shaking when the mother, still wearing her pink scrubs from work, runs to pull her two daughters from their beds and into the kitchen. She tells them to get into the position they've learned at school. Duck and cover. Under the biggest table. Furniture slides across the room and the three of them cling to each other as pictures fall from the walls and glass shatters.

The older one has started to wail first and the little one who always imitates her has joined in, somewhat hollowly, as if she really doesn't understand why she's crying. The woman has to shout to be heard over their cries and the sound of their house combusting around them.

"I love you, my babies," the woman says. "Acacia. Little Lily. You are deep in my heart and I'm in yours. No matter what happens we will never really be apart."

When the older girl comes to, the shaking has stopped. Her house has ceased to exist. The table they hid under is gone. The ceiling is a merciless sky.

Her mother and sister are bleeding. Their eyes are closed. They lie motionless. She places her hands on her mother's head, her always carefully styled black hair. The girl's skin is paler than her mother's and she wishes it weren't. She wishes she at least had that reminder sealing her own body forever.

The blood keeps rivering out while the daughter closes her eyes and focuses every cell of her being on the task of making it stop. Her mother used to say, "Acacia, girl, you have the touch. Someday you're going to be a doctor, I bet. You can make my headaches go away just by putting your little hands on me, baby."

This is not a headache.

The blood stops. But it's too late. Her mother and sister are dead.

The girl rises to her feet and looks around. The water is everywhere. It looks like a sea monster. Leviathan is the word her mother taught her. As the wave comes toward her she clutches a piece of furniture, hauling herself up onto it this time. It's the kitchen table, the one she and her mother and sister hid under as they'd been taught to in the earthquake drills. It hadn't protected them at all.

All lies, the way even her mother's words were lies: We will never really be apart.

The girl clings to the table that betrayed them as it takes her out to sea.

I return from my unwelcome vision. More devastation. Always. Everywhere. We must help this girl.

But right now I can't even walk and she is running up and over the rocks. At the highest point she turns and looks right at Venice, gesturing for him to follow her.

Hex and Venice carry me over the rocks after the girl. A wind smelling of my wounds makes me shiver and I press myself against Hex.

He should drop you down from here and let you die.

I wake up on the ground, next to a burning campfire in the shelter of some rocks. My head is in Ez's lap, Argos is lying somewhere both on and between my feet as he somehow manages to do, and I can hear Ash singing a lullaby. Venice is cross-legged beside me at the entrance to a small cave.

I try to sit up but pain stabs through me. Someone has bandaged my shoulder and probably cleaned it but the wound feels hot, teeming with bacteria.

"She's awake," Ez says to the others.

Venice turns toward me and Ash comes over but I don't see Hex anywhere.

Ez helps lift my head and offers me water from a small bowl. I gulp at it, spilling some down my chin.

"Where are we?" I ask.

"Some island. I don't know exactly."

"What happened?"

"That girl ran off and we followed her."

"Is she okay?" I say. I feel compelled to find this girl, to help her in some way. Venice's eyes tell me he's having the same thought.

"She disappeared so we found water and some berries and made camp." Ez holds up a handful of crushed red berries and I let him feed me, trying to be more careful than with the water. They taste bitter but I don't care. I gulp more water; it seems I'll never get enough.

"What happened before, on the king's island?" The words hurt to pronounce but the silent question in my mind is worse.

"There must have been some kind of spell that was broken when he . . . when he died," Venice says. "The whole island was some kind of enchantment."

He died.

The king died. Burned to death.

Burnt offering.

It was all an enchantment. The harpies were poisoned, decimated girls dressed in rotting feathers; the king transformed them to appear as beautiful winged girls. Why would they have killed him? They said something about me making them do it. Why?

Because you slept with him! Because they wanted him and he betrayed them. Because you betrayed your lover.

"Hex!" I say. "Where's Hex?"

There's silence filled only with the cold salt wind. Then a voice says, "Right here, Queen Penelope."

I still can't see him, but, "I need to talk to you," I say. "In private."

Ez makes clucking sounds, trying to discourage me. *Too weak. Need rest. Not yet. It can wait.*

He must have guessed already. And if he knows, then Hex knows. *Queen Penelope. He knows.* Did I say something before? Why did I speak?

But I have to tell him the truth now that I'm more lucid; it has to come from me.

"Please let us talk alone," I say, coughing. There's a cloud of tobacco on the air. Maybe I'm imagining . . .

Ez makes a pillow out of leaves and eases me down onto it. He and Ash walk away. I notice that they're not touching each other the way they usually do. Venice follows them, looking back at me with his gray eyes, a worried half smile, which means he's afraid. Only Argos stays.

Hex squats down beside me but he doesn't touch me. He's smoking a cigarette and I wonder where he got it. The cigarette is gripped between his fore and middle fingers and he brings it to his lips and rolls his eyes upward as he inhales, not bothering to direct the smoke away from me, even when I cough again.

"Where'd you get that?" I say.

He takes another drag and blows the smoke directly at me this time. "Don't be a hater."

"I just wondered."

"Score, huh? Found them in the cave."

"Are you okay?" I ask him.

"Of course I'm fine," he clips without looking me in the eye. "What's up?"

"I'm sorry I drank the wine. I know that's hard for you."

He smiles and the coldness of it makes me shiver. "Actually, that's not really an issue. Knock yourself out and party." Nodding around us at the dark landscape. "We better live it up while we can, homegirl."

I gulp and take a breath. The pain in my shoulder almost helps; it's like the punishment I deserve. "I need to tell you something. The reason the king was killed. You left me. I thought you were gone."

"Yeah, I wanted to find a way to get us out of there safely?" He says it like a question. "I built a little boat? That's what I was doing with my time while you all went swimming and shit. Or whatever you were doing. So when you got rammed by that spear I had a way to get you the hell out of there."

"But you could have told me."

"Actually, Pen? No. I couldn't. You were drunk, which, you know, is completely fine with me, and high as fuck on King Bucky Horny whatever-his-name-is." Hex pushes up his sweatshirt sleeve and examines the tattoo that reads *Faithless*. "Virgil mentions the Agathyrsi people? They were known for their tattoos, dyeing their hair indigo blue, wearing lots of gold, and taking *multiple wives*."

Hex knows everything. How does he know? Did he guess? Did I tell him?

As usual, he can read my thoughts.

> "'*Rumour, the swiftest traveller of all the ills
>   on earth
> Thriving on movement, gathering strength as it goes,
>   at the start
> A small and cowardly thing, it soon puffs itself up
> And walking upon the ground, buries its head in the
>   cloud-base.
> . . . A swift-footed creature, a winged angel of ruin,
> A terrible, grotesque monster, each feather upon
>   whose body—
> Incredible though it sounds—has a sleepless eye
>   beneath it,
> And for every eye she has also a tongue, a voice and
>   a pricked ear.'*"

It's the passage from *The Aeneid* where the secret liaison between Aeneas and Queen Dido is revealed. "Stop speaking in Virgil. Please, Hex."

> "*But who can ever hoodwink a woman in love?*
>   *The queen*
> *Apprehensive even when things went well, now*
>   *sensed his deception.*'"

"Hex!" In this passage, Queen Dido realizes that Aeneas is leaving her but I know that's not what Hex means by quoting this; he means that I have deceived him and he's right.

"Speaking in Virgil? Wouldn't that be Virgilese, technically? Virgilesque? Virgellian? You like to make up words, remember?" He's returned from his epic reverie and his eyes move over all of me like punishing fingers. "Ez and Ash told me what the harpy things said. About blaming you for them killing him. And I figured the only thing that would have made them kill their precious king was . . ."

"I'm sorry, Hex. I didn't know what I was doing. Please . . ." My pulse is spreading the pain faster through my body. *Good.*

"Yeah, good times, man. My girlfriend forever

partook of bold debauchery, or, in layman's terms, fucked around on me."

"I'm sorry, Hex, I'm so sorry."

"GFN. Girlfriend Never. Girlfriend No More. I like the sound of it."

"Forgive me, please. I don't know how . . ." I reach my hand out to him but he makes a face like he's smelled something rotten—the harpies without their enchantment—and moves farther away.

"I think you do. Basically, it's Copulation 101. You get naked with the antler dude and you spread your legs. Actually the antlers aren't basic. That's a little kinky."

"Stop it. Don't do this!"

"It's not me who did shit," he says. He smiles sweetly, showing his pointed incisors.

"He had control over me," I say. "I swear, Hex. You said yourself. It was a spell."

"None of the rest of us slept with him, though, huh? So he reserved his sex spell just for you?"

"I don't know what he wanted. I don't know why."

"Although from what Ash says, Ez kind of liked him, too. I guess Horny King wasn't into him, though." Hex stretches the sleeves of his sweatshirt down over his fingers, exposing his clavicle. He gets up, dusts dirt off the butt of his jeans, and walks away from our camp.

Don't do this.

But, like he said, it isn't Hex who did anything. My mother, she did this to my father. It's not an excuse but maybe it's part of the reason. It's in me, like bad blood, like the ability to kill that I got from Merk.

But maybe this was different. Merk was my parents' best friend and he and my mom consciously betrayed my father. I didn't know the king at all. I was under his spell. He controlled me; I couldn't say no. I wish I could have made it stop. I couldn't make it stop.

Or maybe any kind of "love" is a spell. You can choose to let it own you. Or not.

"Hex!" I cry with what feels like my last breath. Argos sits up on his hind legs as if on alert.

Hex turns around. He pauses.

A young tree grows nearby and he reaches over and snaps off a branch, tosses it at me. The leaves glim-glint in the moonlight like strange gold.

That dainty, jagged smile again. "Go to hell," Hex says.

I will, I think, as I press my face down into my bed of leaves. I will go straight to hell.

When I open my eyes the little girl is squatting in front of me with her hands on my shoulder. We're in a cave, illuminated only by the glow from her irises, like a cat's. *Tapetum lucidum* is the term for the light-reflecting tissue of the cat's eye, just behind the retina.

I wonder if this is the cave Venice was sitting in front of, the one where Hex found his cigarettes.

"Where's everyone?" I ask.

"Xandra wants me to take you to her."

I'm relieved to see the girl is all right but I need to know where my friends are.

The girl answers, but only cryptically. "Xandra says if I take you to her she'll set us all free."

<hr>

A woman with cropped fair hair is seated in a dark chamber with three huge black dogs surrounding her. Ez, Ash, Venice, and Argos are all there, at her feet. Argos is growling at the dogs as if he thinks he's larger than they are. I don't see Hex.

<hr>

What the girl is saying is true.

"Who's Xandra?" I ask her. I realize that the wound on my arm doesn't hurt anymore; the skin has healed. "Where's your family?"

"My family is gone."

I recall the vision I had when I first saw the girl. A woman with skin darker than hers, wearing a pink nurse's uniform, hiding under a table, trying to shelter her children with her body.

"Xandra is the Queen of the Shades. She lives underground. I have to take you there." The girl's eyes fluoresce, casting a beam of light farther into the darkness, revealing a low, dark tunnel.

Things are starting to add up and I don't like what I think they mean. No pain. Darkness. A journey underground. The disappearance of my loved ones.

"Where are my friends?" I say again.

"If you go to her she won't hurt them," the girl tells me.

"What does that mean?" I can raise my voice now without it hurting to do so, like I'm on some kind of strong medication. Or dead. I press on my shoulder, testing, and don't even wince. "How did my wound heal?"

The girl holds up her hands, palms facing me, stained purple. Petals that same color lie in a pile beside her.

"Did you heal it?"

She nods. Her worried smile reminds me of Venice.

"Thank you for helping me. What's your name?" I ask.

"Acacia."

"Where are you from?"

She shrugs. "There was a sea monster. She looked like a pretty girl but she had a dolphin's tail and a wolf's belly and three blue dogs."

I've seen Giants but I choose to believe that this sea monster is a figment of a child's imagination, a child faced with the loss of her family and (mysteriously, but then again, it's all mystery now) schooled in *The Aeneid*. The sea monster Scylla with her dolphin's tail, wolf's belly, and three "sea-blue hounds" was yet another obstacle Aeneas had to overcome.

"How do you know about Scylla?" I ask.

"My mother read to me and my sister a lot."

"The storm separated you from your mother and sister?" I wish I hadn't asked. The little girl's eyes cloud over as if with the mist that lies on the ocean. "Acacia," I say, "thank you again for healing my arm. Now can you show me how to help my friends? And then we can help you."

She takes my hand and pulls me to my feet; she's incredibly strong. "Come," she says, handing me a branch. I recognize it as the one Hex tossed at me before he left. "We don't have much time."

Go to hell, Hex said. Now it's my chance to go where I deserve to be and maybe save the ones I love if it's not too late.

❧〜❧

This is the journey to hell, down through darkling tunnels, toward the center of the earth. I have to stoop over to fit in the low passageways. I can hear water trickling, smell a sulfur stench, and when I reach out the walls feel jagged and slick with slime. As the little girl leads me down, through corridors of rough rock, I think of all the ways I have sinned. Fighting with my mother, making my little brother cry, not appreciating how hard the man who raised me as his own daughter worked to care for us. All the Chimeras and Gorgons and Centaurs and Furies that I have been parade before me in the darkness. I think of how I stabbed a Giant in the eye and killed two people and now, perhaps worst of all—because the killing was in self-defense—betrayed my lover. I don't really believe in sin or hell but then I never believed that Giants and witches and fairies and harpies and antlered illusionists were real either. I worried about global warming but I didn't really believe the world would end. It's not just me who has sinned, but all of humanity by neglecting the planet.

And then I see him.

He is missing his eyes; his nose and left ear have been cut off. Much like Aeneas's comrade Deiphobus, who was mutilated this way by his wife's lover during the battle of Troy. I know this modern-day incarnation of Deiphobus. He is my father, Merk.

I didn't realize until now how much I still need him.

Who will bring me food in the night? Who will rescue me from monsters?

"Who did this? Why did this happen to you?" I say, forcing myself to look at his ruined face that speaks of all the destruction I have witnessed in these months since the world came to an end. His empty eye sockets like mine. Is that what I look like? Father and daughter.

"The harpies did it in their fury. It is as it was meant to be," he says.

"You're really dead? It's not an illusion this time?" Each word feels like a small shard of glass cutting my throat.

"Yes."

"So we are in hell?"

He frowns. "I prefer to call it the Land of the Shades."

"Then I'm dead?"

"All true heroes have to make a descent to the underworld in order to be reborn" is his cryptic answer. Why is he speaking like an epic hero all of a sudden?

"Staying dead might be better," I say, holding back a sob that threatens to tear through my chest.

"No, it wouldn't. Sometimes it takes a while to realize that what we want isn't what's best. You were meant to be here and to find the king. It's for the greater good."

I stop on the path. A dark mist from the bowels of the earth swirls around us so I can barely see him now.

"What about Hex?" I ask. "What about Hex? Why did I do that to him? Was that meant to be, too? Because you and my mother betrayed my adopted father? Is that why I was cursed to betray Hex?"

"That's not why. And I don't regret what I did, even though it hurt my best friend," he says. "Because if I hadn't been with your mother, you wouldn't have been born."

Then, before he vanishes into the miasma he speaks these last words: "What was also meant to be is your meeting with the Queen of the Shades."

At this, Acacia squeezes my hand as if to urge me on.

I don't know who the Queen of the Shades is but I know I have to go to her and try to redeem myself in some way—save my friends, help this little girl, pay the price. I don't know why I'm allowed underground like this at all, assuming I am even still alive.

When I ask my young guide why I am allowed here, she answers, "Anyone who sets foot on this island is in the in-between." This does not exactly reassure me.

Virgil said it better than anyone as he recounted Aeneas's descent to the underworld:

"The way . . . is easy;
Night and day lie open the gates of death's dark
*   kingdom:*

But to retrace your steps, to find the way back to
  daylight—
That is the task, the hard thing."

That is the task.
There is no choice.

❧ ◡ ❧

The tunnel opens out into a dark cavern dripping with stalactites and lit only by torches. A teenage girl is seated on a chair and surrounded by three low-growling black dogs with one large black-, red-, and yellow-striped snake draping itself around their necks.

I think of Merk's revulsion of the phantom snakes on the ship. I am not a fan of serpents, either.

In contrast to the dark animals, the girl's hair glows like a flock of fireflies, crowning the long sharp angles of her face. As I come closer I see her ice eyes and I remember the vision of the girl in the room with the young king, her brother.

"Xandra the Queen of the Shades," Acacia whispers to me. She hasn't let go of my hand the whole time and I'm surprised my palm is dry, not sticky with sweat.

"Welcome," says Xandra. She's beautiful in a strong, almost masculine way. "I'm glad to finally meet the famous

Queen Penelope." She's smiling but it's a dangerous thing on her face.

"Where am I?" I ask.

"Underground on the Island of the Shades."

"Are you the king's sister? Because I think you aren't alive anymore. And neither are they." Meaning the dogs and the snake.

"Getting right to the point," she says. "I admire that. Yes, I'm Dylan's sister, Xandra. I killed myself when I was sixteen. I couldn't deal with all the pain in the world, and the pain I knew was on its way. Dylan stuck it out. He knew you were coming—something about a picture I made. He devoted his life to you. But look what happened."

"I'm so sorry," I say, aware of the weird lack of pain in my body, even the dull or sharp aches of emotion. It's as if I've sipped from the river Lethe and forgotten what it was like to feel.

"Yes, it was a tragedy. Another tragedy. And now you're here."

I look around the cavern but I can't see past the circle of torchlight where Xandra sits. "Where are my friends?"

"Do you mean the boys? And that yappy dog? They're a motley crew. I have them."

"If you have them . . . does that mean . . . ?"

She grins skeletally. "No, don't worry. They're still

alive for now. At least in part. You all entered the realm of the in-between when you arrived here."

"Please, may I see them?" I say.

"First you must eat something." Xandra points her finger and more torches flare, revealing a table piled with silver platters and crystal bowls of food. Whole fish with shining eyes and garnished with snails and small, gelatinous eggs. Turkeys stuffed to overflowing with sausages. Giant whole grilled fungi. Heaps of pastries oozing cream and bloodred sauce. A great white pig with an apple in her mouth and a litter of piglets surrounding her on the platter.

I'm not exactly hungry or thirsty anymore but I'm drawn to the vile food anyway. I lick my lips. They're very dry and tiny flakes of skin stick to my teeth. I remember the words of the harpies. *If you leave us here you will face famine, fire, and flood.*

Acacia grips my hand tighter, pulling on my arm, and I turn to look at her. She shakes her head very slightly. *No.*

In all the literature I've read about the underworld you must refrain from eating anything or you can never leave. I'm lucky my favorite foods aren't here and for a moment I remember what the king served me at his quartz table.

"No, thank you," I say.

Xandra smiles from under the corona of her pale hair. "Are you sure? You may not realize it but you're very malnourished and you need sustenance. When's the last time you ate a real meal?"

After the king's seafood stew, rice, salad, and wine there's been nothing but the water and crushed bitter berries Ez gave me.

"Because what Dylan gave you?" Xandra says. "That wasn't real. Weeds and roots and acorns maybe if you were lucky. Even the water you drank was enchanted to appear fresh and clear. After the disaster he gained powers for transforming the appearance of things. He had this fixation on you and how he could create what he thought you wanted to see. I still don't understand it."

I think of the island after the king's brutal death. No quartz palace full of oil paintings and silk dresses; no flowers, no fruit trees, no meadows. Just ash and debris and bones and ruin. All the wonder of the island had been a glamour cast by the magician king.

There is no beauty left in the world, I think.

Except for my home, across the sea. But that might be gone now, decimated by Bull. And more important, my friends, my little family—the truest beauty—they might be gone as well.

"I want to see my friends," I say. "I'm willing to stay here if you let them go. And her, too." I nod at Acacia.

Xandra taps her lips with one finger. "Very nice. Self-sacrifice. A hero's trait." She frowns in a way that reminds me of the king. "Fair enough."

She motions for Acacia to come forward and the little girl drops my hand and walks over to her.

"Go bring them here," Xandra says.

Acacia looks back at me, the lenses of her eyes glowing green planets in her dusky face, and then she runs off into the darkness.

I guess I'm not entirely dead or drunk on Lethe because when Acacia returns and I see Ez, Ash, and Venice holding Argos I feel something stirring in the cavity of my chest. But I don't run to them the way I normally would and they don't come to me either. Xandra's eyes seem to be waiting to catch any sign of indiscretion.

Argos growls at the black dogs and they calmly turn their heads toward him and bare their teeth. Any of them could snap him up in one bite. Venice struggles to keep him quiet.

"Where's Hex?" I ask.

"The one who likes Virgil. We've been sharing quotes. We'll see if you deserve Hexane or not. Now remember, you haven't eaten or even had much water for longer than you realize. Make yourself at home.

"Oh, one other thing. I thought you'd like this quote Hex and I have been discussing. It's about the death of

Queen Dido who killed herself when her lover betrayed her. Not exactly apropos of our situation here but there are similarities." She puts her hand to her breast and when she speaks again her eyes glitter ferally and her mouth slathers spittle.

> "*Not yet had Proserpine clipped from her head*
> *The golden tress, or consigned her soul to the*
> *   Underworld,*
> *So now, all dewy, her pinions the color of yellow crocus,*
> *Her wake a thousand rainbow hues refracting the*
> *   sunlight,*
> *Iris flew down, and over Dido hovering, said:——*
> *As I was bidden, I take this sacred thing, the*
> *   Death-god's*
> *Due: and you I release from your body.*
> *She snipped the tress.*
> *Then all warmth went at once, the life was lost in air.*"

"But Dido killed herself," I say, meeting her gaze though it makes my stomach churn. "The king was killed by the harpies."

"And I blame you for that. He slept with you and they found out and became jealous."

"But if you were able to haunt that ship, if you were

able to make me and Hex find our own corpses, why couldn't you save him?" I ask her.

Xandra raises her arm and the torches around her flare and go out. When they flame up again she's gone and so is Acacia. The dogs and snake are still there.

Now my friends come forward, surrounding me. I close my eyes and we all sink to the ground in a heap, huddling together, restraining brave little Argos from attacking the dogs.

"Are you okay? Tell me what's going on," I say.

"We were separated from you and we searched and then finally fell asleep. I'm sorry, Pen. When we woke up we were here," Venice says. I can tell he's holding back tears.

I kiss his forehead. "It's okay. Look. Acacia healed my shoulder."

Venice puts his hand where my wound was.

"Acacia." He speaks her name shyly, almost with longing, looking into the dark where she stood moments before.

How people come and go in this new world.

I have always only seen the past but as I follow Venice's gaze into the dark I glimpse a vision of an older Venice—so tall now, he's finally had his growth spurt. Maybe he's eighteen? Broad

shouldered, lightly bearded; he's standing beside an older Acacia with a pregnant belly. They are holding hands and wearing crowns of golden leaves. Around their feet kneel young women with skin conditions, broken limbs, all kinds of maladies, waiting to be healed by Venice's wisdom and Acacia's hands.

King and Queen of the world that is to come. Maybe it's real; maybe it's my hopeful dreaming.

But where are the rest of us?

Eventually, you may be able to see into the future as well, *the king had said.*

"What about Hex?" I ask Venice. I won't tell him yet about the vision I've just seen, although judging by the way he was looking at Acacia I don't think he'd be surprised by it.

"We haven't seen him. He ran off after you talked to each other," says Ez. "I followed him for a while. He didn't see me. He was crying. Then he started to run and I was worried about you so I went back and I lost him."

Hex, crying!

"Do you think he's here?" I ask. "And where are we anyway?"

Ez puts his arm around me. "Xandra says that this island rose up from the sea after the Earth Shaker."

"She's the king's sister," Venice says. "The Queen of the Shades."

"That's true," I tell him. "I mean that she's dead and the king's sister. I saw it."

"If she's the queen of the dead, then are we . . ." Venice starts to ask.

"We're not dead." I don't know if it's true but I have to say this in order not to give up, to keep Venice and the others from giving up.

"All I know is I'm starving." Ez eyes the food. "I could eat the table."

"Don't. Remember your mythology? You can never leave the underworld if you eat anything there," I tell him.

"I mean the table itself. Do you think there are any rules about not eating furniture in the underworld?" I remember the harpy's curse: *Your hunger will gnaw at you until you eat the furniture and when that is not enough you will eat each other.* Ez is still staring at the food now and I recall how I first met him in Beatrix the witch's demolished mansion. She'd gained control over him with sweets. He's the one I have to watch the closest now.

Ez stands and walks unsteadily toward the table.

"Don't," Ash says, jumping to his feet. But Ez keeps walking as if he doesn't hear him.

"Ez!" I shout, standing too. My body is like a hollow

gourd. I wonder if food would make me feel human or if it's too late for that.

Would it be so bad to have to stay here forever? At least the five of us are together and the alternative—to return to that forsaken island—isn't much better. And maybe we really are dead, in which case we'll have to stay anyway.

I can smell the roasted meat and burnt sugar wafting off the food.

Argos twists himself in Venice's arms and Venice shouts and Argos leaps away from him, not toward the dogs but onto the table.

Where he relieves himself all over the feast.

Gross. Nasty. What the hell? Everyone's talking at once but I'm proud of my dog. He did the right thing. I get up and take him in my arms, hugging his body, scratching him behind the ears so he lets down his guard and allows his eyes to close in pleasure for a moment. Back on duty he looks at the black hounds, the low growl resuming in his throat so I can feel it reverberating through his body.

"Damn!" Ez collapses against a wall of the cavern. "I really wanted some of that cake."

Ash goes to him and takes him in his arms. His voice is softer than I've heard it since before we left home. "I know you did."

Ez blinks at him. "I'm so sorry," he says.

"It's okay."

"I mean on the Island of Excess Love. I didn't see clearly."

"I know. Neither did I. That wine was good, though."

"It wasn't even real." Ez sighs, leans into Ash, and closes his eyes. Ash kisses the top of his head. "I don't even want to know what we really ate and drank there."

Ash nods to the disgusting feast before us. "It couldn't have been worse than that."

"Let's rest," Venice says. "We can't do anything more tonight."

"I'll keep watch awhile," I say. Still holding Argos tight I slump down beside Ez and Ash on the cold rock floor. Venice joins us and they all sleep. When I can't keep my eyes open anymore I wake Ash, ask him to take a turn, and hand Argos over.

Later, when Ash wakes me, someone is sitting in the darkest recesses of the cavern.

"It's Hex," Ash whispers.

Yes, I'm still alive. I may not feel hunger or thirst or pain but I feel this. I feel Hex. My guilt at what I did, my terrible remorse and longing. Or maybe this is just the punishment of hell—to feel only this for eternity.

Argos strains in Ash's arms, trying to get to Hex. He comes over and takes Argos from Ash, letting the dog kiss his neck and face. Fastidious Hex usually doesn't allow this.

"Hey, little man. Did you miss me?" He sounds gentle and I look up hopefully, but when he catches my eye his gaze turns cold as the stone of the cave. He gives Argos back to Ash.

"Where were you?" Ash asks.

"Around. This place sucks. That lady is a psycho but at least she gives me cigarettes." He pulls one out and lights it on a torch, the cherry sizzling in the dark cavern.

Ez and Venice are blinking awake. The black dogs are still watching us. Their upper lips are drawn back; I can see the edges of their white teeth.

The torches go out and then flare.

Xandra and Acacia are there again, Xandra in her chair and Acacia seated in her lap, letting the older girl braid her hair. Acacia seems to be trying to make eye contact with me, to tell me something, but I can't decipher it. Except that it's some kind of warning.

"Very good," Xandra says to us. "You've passed the test and now you've received your reward." She smiles at Hex but he ignores her, jamming his hands in the pocket of his filthy hoodie. I realize he's probably worn it since before we set sail on the ghost ship. He was too proud to accept the king's clothes, but they weren't real anyway; they were rags held together with thorns, like the tatters I'm still wearing, glamoured by a spell.

"So will you let us leave now?" I ask.

"Not yet. There's one more test. Well, maybe a few actually." Xandra gently pushes Acacia off her lap. "Go get him," she says.

Acacia runs off. We wait. I try to get Hex to look at me but he refuses. His shoulders are stooped as if he's trying to keep someone from stealing his precious cigarette, and he looks thinner than ever.

I wonder if Hex will ever forgive me, if there's anything I can say or do. We didn't have to get sent to hell; I'd already made my own. I think of him crying and I wish he could have shown me those tears instead of his anger. Then maybe I could have reached him. Will I spend eternity trying to repair the damage I have wreaked?

Acacia returns holding the hand of a figure covered in a robe with a hood.

"This is my brother, the revenant king, Dylan."

He reaches out his other hand to me and I see that the skin is charred black.

I fall to my knees before him with the force of shock.

"I'm so sorry," I say.

He nods his hood but doesn't speak. His sister is looking at me in a curious way. I realize how similar their faces are—high cheekbones; straight, long nose; angular chin. Their faces *were*. Oh, my king.

"Can you do anything?" I ask Acacia, taking her free hand, running my fingers over the palm.

She holds her hand up toward the king, then drops her head and looks away.

"This is how he will always be," Xandra says. "My handsome brother. This is your doing."

I ignore her and address only him. "What happened?"

When he finally speaks his voice is frail. "The harpies were jealous of our relationship. On their pyre I was turned to ash and my ashes blew away on the wind. They came here where I was resurrected. Such as I am. By my sister."

"She could have prevented it," I tell him. "She has strong magic."

The king turns his hooded head to Xandra. She lifts her chin and glares back at him. Her body is so tense that I bet she's shaking, though imperceptibly.

"Penelope is right. Tell me why you didn't prevent my death, Xandra," the king says.

"I did not wish for your death. Your own servant girls killed you out of jealousy. You should never have cast those spells on them to begin with. When I saw in my mind what they were doing to you I decided to let you come to me. I've missed you all these years. And she doesn't deserve you."

"We'll discuss this later," the king says. "You have me. Let her go."

"Please," I say. "We have work to do in the world above." The words surprise me and only when I say them do I realize how true they are and how significant.

Xandra gestures for Acacia and hauls her back onto her lap, undoing the braids she'd made earlier. She's preoccupied with this for what feels like a long time and I wonder if she's forgotten the king's question. Finally she says, almost to herself, "Why should I help these people?"

"As she said, they have work to do," the king answers.

Xandra releases Acacia and waves her hand at Venice. He steels himself, setting his shoulders and staring straight ahead, the way he used to when going up to bat in a baseball game where everything depended on his hit, and goes to her. (I try not to picture his head-hanging stance of defeat when he missed the ball.) "This one is lovely, so charming. A little like you as a child. I'll let him live. But why the rest?"

The king points at Ez. "Ezra paints," he says. "He could paint your portrait, so everyone would know you."

Xandra cocks her head to the side. "Really? Show me."

Acacia gives Ez a piece of parchment and a jar of ink,

probably made from a combination of charcoal, powdered stone, and gum arabic like the ancients used. He kneels on the floor and begins to sketch Xandra. As always, it's a perfect representation of her form, with only the slightest exaggerations to make her even more compelling.

A bemused smile gentles the corners of her mouth. "Not bad."

The king points to Ash. "Ash sings. Sing for her, Ash."

Ash stands straighter and looks at Xandra. He begins to sing. It's a song from Then I can't quite place, something in a foreign language. Maybe Icelandic? Almost religious sounding. Dirgelike. I've forgotten how much I love Ash's songs. His voice seems to reach down inside me, bringing me back to life.

Xandra nods but I think I see a tear in her eye. Maybe it's just the light. She's looking at Hex now. "And what about him?"

"Hexane?" The king's voice has changed so much since the last time I heard him utter this name. He hesitates and I bite down on the inside of my lip. What if the king doesn't feel Hex is worth saving?

Hex pulls out a cigarette from his pocket and dangles it from his mouth, fierce eyes on Xandra.

"Hexane is a fighter," the king says.

"Show me."

Xandra holds out a sword. It's forged of metal with

crystals embedded in the hilt. The king bows his hooded head and gestures for Hex to take the sword.

But before we actually see this exchange Hex is poised in front of Xandra and the tip of the sword has pierced her chest.

I gasp.

Hex pulls the sword out. There's no blood anywhere, not even a tear in Xandra's garment. She looks down at her chest and smiles.

"Very nice work. You are a fighter, young man."

"What about Penelope?" Venice says. His voice is clear and strong. He looks into Xandra's eyes without flinching.

"What about Penelope, Dylan?" Xandra says. "I know you think she is your destiny but all that's over now."

"Penelope is a hero. She is self-sacrificing, disciplined, noble, brave, clever, and a storyteller."

"An epic storyteller," Hex adds, under his breath but loud enough so only I can hear. "Epic. Fail."

Xandra wrinkles her nose like a petulant child. "I've seen some of this. I'm not sure it's enough."

"There's one other thing." The king walks over to his sister, leans forward, and whispers something into her ear.

Xandra stares at me for such a long time that I have to fight not to look away. "I didn't believe you were the one," she says. "That you were meant to return this wretched planet to its former state. My brother always believed it but I didn't. It was I who made you and your friends mad on that ship Dylan sent for you, peopled it with ghosts to drive you insane. It was I who showed you the bleeding branch and your dead bodies. I wanted to discourage you from finding my brother, make you turn away in terror, but you would not give up and, as I feared, you destroyed him."

"I didn't mean for any of this to happen."

"I knew you would ultimately be the cause of his destruction."

"You were the cause of his destruction!" I can't contain the rage in my voice.

"No, I only allowed the inevitable to happen, the harpies to kill him. I finally accepted his fate and allowed him to come to me."

"But the ship, the corpses. Why did you do that to my friends and me? You could have kept us from coming without tormenting us."

"Actually, I thought you'd be grateful for that. Consider it a warrior's training. Facing her own madness. Burying her old self so her new self may be reborn. Even though you passed these tests, I never believed you were the chosen one. Now my brother the king has made it true."

What did he say to her?

Hex flashes a glance at me. It burns like fire, singeing the hairs that are standing up on my arms.

"I will consider your request," Xandra says. "I will give you one more night and then I will decide."

The torches go out and when they flare again she and Acacia and the king are gone.

The dogs are blocking the single exit from the cave, the snake draped like a collar around their necks. I squat down and look into their eyes.

Three black puppies in a basket in front of a supermarket. The girl is going in to buy groceries for her mother. She sees the puppies and kneels by the basket. There is a sign that says FREE. *The puppies are huddled so close they look like one dog with three heads until the smallest one sniffs the girl's fingers and then hops up on hind legs to kiss her face. The others are too listless with hunger and thirst to move. She strokes their heads, the velvety indentations on their brows.*

"Cerberus," she says. She touches each one as she names them.

"Sir. Burr. Us? No, Uzi."

She picks up the basket and carries the dogs home. Later she goes back to the supermarket for groceries and dog food.

She bathes and feeds them and lets them sleep on her bed.

The next day she takes them for their inoculations but doesn't have them neutered because it sounds too barbaric. She treats them like her own babies and they are devoted to her. Sometimes she wonders if they think she is their mother.

It is for this reason, in part, that she poisons them when she kills herself. So as not to leave them alone. But also, she wants their company when she descends to the underworld. She does not want to be alone either.

But what does this mean for these strong, healthy young dogs? And the snake that ties their throats?

It means a life under the ground; it means darkness; it means becoming guardians of the damned.

Argos was in Venice's arms but somehow he's escaped. He is running toward the dogs. I try to stop him but trip and fall on the slimy rock. When I look up Argos is standing in front of the dogs, barking up at them. All three lower their heads and back away, making a mewling sound.

"I think we can leave," Venice says.

I place my hand between his shoulder blades. "Go!"

Venice scoops up Argos and dashes toward the tunnel that leads back up.

"You too," I say, pushing Ez and then Ash.

I wait for Hex but he only looks at me coolly. He

holds up the sword the king gave him and for a second I'm afraid he might strike me with it. But his only attack is with his eyes and voice. "Get out of here."

"You're coming, though?"

Hex shrugs. "Exchange one hell for another?"

"But at least we'll have each other," I say. "So everything will be okay."

"How?" His voice is softer now. I can almost imagine this Hex in tears.

"Because I love you," I say. "And that's all we really ever have."

He shakes his head. No.

So I take off into the recesses of the tunnel, praying against all the odds that Hex is following, afraid to look back and discover that he has disappeared.

In the myth of Orpheus, when his beloved Eurydice was bitten by a snake and taken to the underworld, he had to go below to rescue her, using the charm of his music to lead her back up. But doubting, he looked back and lost her. Even the power of love and art, the two greatest powers that we have, cannot always save us. The black-glistening walls of the tunnel are telling me: death is more powerful.

Don't look back, Pen.

Cold sweat is slicking my body and it's hard to

breathe in the close space of the tunnel. I can't tell if I'm ascending at all; the climb is incremental and there are no steps, only rough rock hollowed out, perhaps, by the flow of ancient waters. How did Orpheus feel as he returned without his beloved wife? He was ripped to shreds by the wild women, the maenads, when he emerged. Perhaps he was grateful for being put out of his misery.

If maenads tore me to pieces I might not even feel it, so dead am I already.

When I arrive above ground Ez, Ash, Venice, and Argos are waiting for me. We embrace in the cold wind. Saltwater spray clings to my face.

"Where's Hex?" Venice says.

I don't want to turn around. What if I sent Hex to hell? What if he will never return? That's a worse hell for me than being chained with him to Xandra's ankles for eternity. At least if we were together down below, I could tell him how sorry I am forever.

"We have to go," Ash says softly into my ear. "If the boat's still there. He can catch up with us."

When he and Ez put their arms around me I remember that the wound on my shoulder has healed. *Acacia the healer.* If only my heart could be mended this easily.

We make our way over the rocks. Someone has built a kind of city out of trash. Tall clay columns are inlaid with bottle caps, broken glass, shattered china, mechanical parts, pieces of plastic toys. Dismembered furniture is arranged as if for some mad tea party. Plastic bottles are lined up in a row, as if for our taking. So we take as many as we can carry.

We move on, toward a grove of small young saplings. There's a pool of fresh water and we all fall to our knees and slurp until our stomachs can hold no more. I wonder how we survived so long underground, without food, or water especially, after having only phantom food and water on the Island of Excess Love. Maybe we really were dead for a while.

We fill the bottles with water, gather berries, leave the trees, and head for the sea. Our small boat is there, waiting, moored to a rock.

Ash and Ez get in first and take up the oars. I get in and Venice goes last with Argos. We hesitate for a moment, staring at the rocky island with its tide pools and new young growth, its mysterious trash city. I know we're all thinking the same thing.

Hex.

"Maybe we should wait for him overnight," I say.

"They might come after us." Ez's shoulders shudder. In a softer voice he says, "He's made his choice."

"No! I made a choice. And it was the wrong one. And I lost him because of it." I'm trying not to cry but it's pretty hopeless.

I rub at my eyes and when I open them again Argos's tail is wagging. I look toward where his nose is pointing, reading the stories of the air. Nothing. What does he smell?

And then I see Hex coming over the rocks, stumbling, running, wielding the sword the king gave to him. I stand in the boat and call his name.

Orpheus never really came back from the dead, but not so for Persephone, or Proserpine as she is called in *The Aeneid*, who became queen of the underworld. She was abducted and brought there by Hades but her mother, the earth goddess Demeter, was able to get her back for half the year, so that she could restore spring to the earth. In this myth love won over death, at least by half.

Hex and I were dead once, corpses on the Island of Excess Love. Now we are reunited, if tenuously. In this moment I imagine our graves on that island, the ones we dug for each other and ourselves. The graves are empty. We are here. We are alive.

As Hex jumps into the boat, avoiding the help of my outstretched hand, and Ez and Ash begin to paddle away, I see a group of figures coming over the rocks toward the beach. There are six young men and six young women, of different skin tones, their lower bodies draped in animal skins, their chests bare, wreaths of leaves in their long wind-whipped hair. Six of them are on the backs of white horses and the others so sure-footed on the rocks, it is as if their feet are cloven hooves.

The island has risen out of the sea. It is still young; the trees are small. Mostly the landscape is just rocks. There is trash on the shore, from the ocean. When the twelve arrive here—washed up from various places and in different ways, but all similarly broken—they know they have been saved for something but they have no idea what it could be.

Running, running, always running. They've lost their families, their homes, everything. Half naked, they keep running, over the rocks until their bleeding feet toughen like horn. Finding fresh water, finding nuts and berries and small animals to eat, finding each other, forming a band of wild folk. Six white horses come to them one night as they are sleeping, standing there in the dawn like a dream, allowing themselves to be mounted and ridden over the rocky landscape. The Fauns and the Nymphs the young men and women call themselves. They gather the trash they find on the island. Each piece reminds them of the sins of their lost world. They try to make it into something of use and beauty.

They begin to forget the time when they thought they were dead. Riding their white horses across the island where purple flowers have begun to grow, they wonder if the twelve of them may actually be alive.

Until that ghost girl, the Queen of the Shades with her three black dogs, the one who summoned them in the first place, makes herself known to them.

Just as when I first saw Acacia I know that these young men and women need us. As they stop and stand on the rocks, watching, the sun beginning to sink behind them, there is a desperation in their eyes that I know well. I had that look, too, until I returned to my home and was reunited with my loved ones.

"They need our help," I say but everyone pretends not to hear me, except for Venice.

"We'll come back someday," he says. He's not looking at me, though. His eyes are on the small girl who has broken through the formation of twelve young men and women and is running toward the boat.

It's Acacia.

She dives into the water and swims toward us, disconcertingly fast. Venice goes to the side of the boat and reaches out for her. He takes her hand and hauls her in.

I can hear the chattering-ring of her teeth and I put my arms around her.

"She can't come. We don't have room," Hex says.

Venice faces him. My brother has grown taller and he is already nearing Hex's height. "She helped us."

"How? By taking us to the Queen of the Damned, there? We don't have room for one more hungry, miserable stray." He flings up his hands. "You all keep bringing more along for the ride."

"She healed Pen's arm," Venice tells him.

Hex glares at me. "Awesome. Really great. She healed Pen's arm."

"Shut up," Venice mumbles.

Hex's whole body registers surprise; Ven has never talked back to him. I expect a response but Hex is quiet.

Acacia escapes my embrace and leans over the side of the boat. She holds up one hand toward the young men and women on the shore.

"Who are they?" I ask her. The torch-smoke scent of her hair is still in my nostrils.

"The brothers and sisters," she says in a small voice, through the chattering.

"What do they want?" Their fervently poised bodies haunt my retina even though I've turned away. I know what they want, but I need to hear Acacia say it.

"They want you to come back here one day, and rescue them from the Island of the Shades."

"Fucking great. Let's just ask them to come along, too," Hex says. "And hey, the horses might fit on our boat if we all pile up."

"Just stop," says Venice, not mumbling now.

Hex is silent and Ez and Ash row the boat farther out to sea away from the twelve figures on the shore. The sky flares red with the setting sun's last cry.

Something rips at my insides and I wonder if this is what my mother felt when she was separated from me as the earth shook. I shouldn't feel this way but I do.

Island of Bone, Sea of Blood. Someday I'll return to you.

Later Hex and I are at the oars. Ash with his knowledge of the currents of air and Ez who understands the earth were able to discern the longitudes and latitudes and point the boat toward home. Now they and Argos are sleeping and Venice and Acacia are at the helm, phosphorescent beams from her eyes lighting the way over the night sea. I didn't want to row with Hex but Venice called us all to take a turn and somehow, after standing up to Hex, my brother has become our captain. I think of him in the vision I had and I'm not surprised by who he is now or who I'm sure he will become.

Hex and I are silent for a long time, the waves and

wind our only form of conversation. My arms feel weak, as if they're made of wind-shaken leaves, but I know I can't give in to the exhaustion, nor can I afford to use up too much energy by speaking.

"I'm sorry," I say to Hex finally, unable to contain myself, and my voice blows away on the cold wind, blows into the firmament, but I keep talking, louder now. "I will say it forever until you hear me."

He doesn't answer.

"Will you ever acknowledge my apology?" I plead, biting back a sob. "Is there anything I can do? Ever?"

Silence.

My words are useless. But maybe Virgil's will have power, and there are some I remember. They are Dido's words when she begs her mistress to help her find a love spell to win Aeneas back. Although Hex, not I, was betrayed like Dido, I wonder if these words will touch him.

"I have been in touch with a priestess . . . who
        once . . . was used to
    Feed the dragon which guarded their orchard of
        golden apples,
    sprinkling its food with moist honey and sedative
        poppy-seeds.
    Now this enchantress claims that her spells can liberate

> One's heart, or can inject love-pangs, just as she
>   wishes;
> Can stop the flow of rivers, send the stars flying
>   backwards,
> Conjure ghosts in the night: she can make the earth
>   cry out
> Under one's feet, and elm trees come trooping down
>   from the mountains."

"Not bad Virgilese," Hex allows. " 'Inject love-pangs.' "

"Yes."

We row through until dawn, the stars disappearing, the sun rising as if it's erupting from the core of the earth. I blink into the red light streaking the horizon.

I wish I could inject love-pangs into Hex's heart and send the stars flying backwards. Why did I share a bed with the king of the Island of Excess Love? Even if I was under a spell, what I did was wrong. I would not be able to forgive Hex if he did the same thing to me. And yet . . . And yet, somehow it feels inevitable. But is that only an excuse for my betrayal?

"Do you know the color blue never existed in ancient times?" Hex says, startling me so that I almost stop rowing. He's addressing me? It's not exactly an acceptance of my apology but at least he's speaking.

I gather myself and register what he's just said. "What do you mean it never existed? What about the sky? And the sea?"

"It went unnamed in the ancient texts. Homer said the 'wine-dark sea,' never once 'the blue sea.'"

"Maybe he was just avoiding clichés," I try to joke. Hex ignores me. "What about blue eyes?" I try not to remember the king's.

"It's not in the literature. Anywhere. Until later," he says. "Virgil says indigo-colored rain cloud, for example, and 'dark-blue chariot.' But not Homer. If you see something all the time, if it's omnipresent, you don't have to name it."

"I don't understand."

"Sometimes we don't see what's most constant and beautiful around us. We take it for granted."

He's trying to tell me something. My heart feels like an empty amphora filling with the nectar of relief. "Yes," I say. "And when it's gone, and night comes, or an Earth Shaker, it's hard sometimes to imagine that a blue sky ever existed at all."

He motions toward the sky over our heads. "A little gray now, but there it is."

"And here you are," I say.

We're silent again. I don't know if this was just a brief

reprieve; I imagine so. What can I say to keep him engaged?

Venice comes over with bottles of water and some berries. The smell of the juice makes my mouth water but my stomach is queasy. I suppose it's from the motion of the boat. "Are you guys okay?"

"Fine."

"Really?"

"Getting a little tired, I guess," I admit.

Hex grunts and my brother goes to wake Ez and Ash.

"Thanks for taking the shift," Ez says as I stand, stretching out my cramped limbs, and hand him my oars. "You feel all right?"

"Hex spoke to me," I whisper. Even saying it makes my heart fill again.

"What did he say?"

"Um, that blue never existed in ancient times?"

"What the hell? Blue's a primary color. Of course it did."

"He has some theory about not seeing what's there all the time."

Ez frowns. "I guess he was trying to make a point."

"I guess."

"At least he talked."

Ash has taken Hex's place and I watch Hex move

toward the stern of the boat. His shoulders are hunched as if he's protecting his heart and his black hair falls over his face, the way, when he held me, it once fell over mine.

"Go talk to him some more," Ez says.

I feel like a thirteen-year-old getting boyfriend advice, which I never did since I liked girls and didn't want anyone to know. If I'd had Ez around I would have talked to him. "What should I say?"

"Remember when Venice said that thing about storytelling helping us see the outcome?"

That seems so long ago, back at the pink house, before the ghost ship and the Island of Excess Love and the Island of the Shades, the death of the king, the death of Merk, whose body I was not even able to bury. The death of Hex's trust in me.

Is grief like the blue of the sky and sea? You can't even see it anymore when it's all you have come to know.

But the king said, "Storytelling helps determine action."

"Tell Hex a story, storyteller," says Ez. "Tell us all a story. We need one."

12

THE RETURN

THIS IS THE STORY I tell them. I don't know for sure if my visions of the future are true, but this is what I see:

When my friends and I arrive home we pray to whatever deities we may still have a shred of belief in, that the pink house is intact, protected by some fog-spell, like the one Venice once used to keep himself from being found out, so the Giant did not see it.

The six of us and Argos drag ourselves up the shore. It is our hope that sustains us; we are weak from so long without food and much water. The feasts at the Island of Excess Love were not real, only scraps enchanted to resemble stews and cakes and wine. Wine did not make us drunk; it was the magic of the king that did that.

But the magic of the king burned with him. Venice could not have hidden a whole house from a Giant, even if he had the opportunity to focus on this feat during the journey to the Shades and back again.

The pink house is ruined.

The whole facade is gone so it resembles the dollhouse I used to play with as a child. The father who raised me made it and I liked to preside over that tiny world, where every choice was mine. But now I am as powerless as the dolls I played with.

Windows are smashed, walls have crumbled, the roof has caved in. The garden has been trampled, destroyed. The Giant is nowhere to be seen and if my friends and I were not so weak with hunger and devastation we would register gratitude for this.

Only the water in the spring is clear-bright as always, tasting of leaves and sunshine. This is still hallowed ground. We fall to our knees in supplication to the dryads and drink.

A few rogue dandelions grow by the spring and we eat the leaves, chewing slowly, savoring the bitter tang. Then we go back to the house, Hex leading us with his sword drawn.

Hex, Ez, Ash, Acacia, and Venice holding Argos tiptoe

over the creaking floorboards and up what is left of the staircase. I take up the rear, glancing back behind me as I go. There is nowhere for a Giant to hide but we still proceed with caution and our hearts startle at every sound. A monster could appear or the stairs could collapse beneath us but we need to survey the extent of the damage.

When night comes we arm ourselves with kitchen knives and huddle together in the large downstairs room where there is the most shelter in spite of the cracked window and the fallen partition that once separated the space into a living and dining area. Hex refuses to rest and keeps watch, pacing the muddy ground in front of the house. I hold Argos, breathing the comfort of his musty fur, and cry myself to sleep as quietly as possible so as not to worry the others.

In the morning we eat more dandelion greens and drink the water and practice our meditations and exercises. When evening comes, Venice calls a meeting and we gather around a fire built in the remains of the fireplace. I sit between Ez and Ash with Argos on my lap, Acacia sits beside Venice, where she seems to always place herself now, and Hex hovers on the outskirts as usual.

"We've all been through a lot," Venice says. "But we can't give up. We can't run away again."

Acacia nods her head, her gaze attaching to his face.

"What are we supposed to do?" Ez asks.

"If Bull comes back we're fucked," Ash adds.

"Not if we have a plan."

We all look at the dove-eyed boy.

"Tell us your plan, Venice," I say.

But there is no time for a plan.

The earth shakes with titanic footsteps and we rush from the house as the remaining walls threaten to cave in. Coming toward us from across the ruined land is the blind Giant, Bull, and two almost identical, half-naked Giantesses. They are, for me, my rage and grief and fear. Rage at my blindness—my eye stolen from me, a bargain made and not kept. Grief at the death of so many of my loved ones. Fear of my own betrayal, of Hex's inability to forgive me. These things must be overcome if my friends and I are to survive.

We stand armed with our knives and Hex's single sword, facing the mottled-cheese flesh and rapacious blood maws of the monsters.

In this moment I remember that my small army and I are not just starving, orphaned boys and girls, lost on a destroyed planet. Not victims. We are heroes in our own ways. We are visionaries and warriors and healers and summoners of the elements.

My hair does not stand up chillily on my head; my voice does not stick meatily in my throat.

"This is our home," I say in a voice both clear and strong,

for I am a warrior, my birth father Merk's fearless daughter.
"You have to leave." I would like to tell them a story to convince
them but these Giants are not interested in tales, they cannot be
soothed by words. They have grown too brutal for that. And, for
now at least, so have I.

One of the Giantesses reaches down and plucks Venice by
his collar, dangling him there, then depositing him into Bull's
hand. I watch my brother disappear in that mitt of flesh and I
become a mother wolf protecting her cub. A wolf starved to shaking, ragged, and blinded but refusing to be vanquished. Seeing
in her mind's eye her endangered wolfling. I am empowered by
what Virgil calls "the fury of desperation." A battle howl erupts
from my throat like a flock of black birds.

Ash climbs up the rickety remains of the house and leaps
from it onto the nearest Giantess's back as if he is flying, for
Ash is a master of air. The female Giant whips around, bellow-
lowing, swatting at him, but he eludes her. Jabs at her with his
knife, perforating her flesh with bloody holes.

Argos runs forward and digs his teeth into Bull's homun-
culus of a toe.

Hex spears Bull's foot with the sword the king gave to him.

The Giants' rage makes their bodies heavier and the earth
opens and swallows, taking them down into a sinkhole. Venice
and Ash and Argos and Hex are with them.

The waters rise up and the waves roll in from the beach,

threatening to drown the Giants in their hellhole. Venice and Ash and Argos and Hex are still trapped there, too.

Then the king comes to me as he once appeared, with his jasmine-twined antlers and his uncharred flesh.

"Words are not your only gift," he says. "Whether you want it or not, you are action as much as word. And now you must protect not only yourself and your loved ones but what remains of me, in you."

Not questioning the greater meaning of these words, I close my eyes and lift my face to the sky and reach out my arms. I call on the great seas to hear me. Those seas that protected and hid the secret worlds, that readied themselves against the devastation they saw being wreaked on their shores, preparing for the aquatic reign of the earth.

The seas will hear. The wave will stop.

And then another Giant appears, storming toward the fray. Kutter, the one who was not too brutal to listen to my story, the Giant who listened, and spared my life.

He reaches down and plucks Venice and Ash and Argos and Hex up with his mighty hand and deposits them back on the solid ground.

Ez closes the earth over Bull and the Giantesses because Ez, who sometimes seems to fear his own shadow, is a master of earth.

Hex, who is the king of fire, and more than this—the king

of my cloven heart—sets a ring of flame around the pit where the Giants are trapped.

This is how they will be sent to hell and how, finally, when I am forgiven by my beloved, I will return from there.

Hex opens his eyes and I realize he has been awake and listening the whole time. I'm not sure if I'm relieved or afraid.

"Pen the storyteller," he says. I'm trying to deter mine if I hear a trace of sarcasm in his tone. "Are you a seeress of the future now, too? Is that what will happen?"

"If we make it happen."

"And what about the end? Where I forgive you. How will that happen?" His voice sounds weary now, and he looks out across the sea.

The ceaseless motion of the boat is making me queasy. It must be from that. It must be.

"You left me," I say to Hex, trying to smack the intrusive thought out of my mind. "I didn't know you would return. I was under a spell. You've been drunk and high, you know what it's like."

He shrugs and pats his imaginary pockets as if searching for a cigarette. "Good times."

"Hex! Stop. You know what I'm saying."

Maybe I've reached him because he finally looks me in the eye. "I'm sorry. I was cruel to you. I left without explaining. But Pen, you . . . you were my source of loyalty." His voice cracks. "Purity and truth. I couldn't stand to see you any other way. I love you too much."

"We're the same," I tell him. "In our imperfection. In our illusions. And in our love."

"I renounce all illusions," says Hex.

"But this is real, what we have."

Hex and I gaze at each other for a long time and I see his eyes fill with tears, mirroring mine. I brace myself to hear him say, *Was real*, but he doesn't.

"Land ho," Venice calls from the prow. Acacia throws her arms around him and Argos, responding to their shouts, twists in joy-spun circles at their feet.

There, I see it. Across the water. What remains of our home. Waiting to be reclaimed and rebuilt.

The pink house stands again. It glows with dawn. Wine-dark morning glories grow up the walls and over the roof. I am sleeping in my old bedroom, in my bed. A sword hangs on the wall.

Where is Hex?

A baby is crying.

I get up and go to the basket where he sleeps. I lift him in my arms and take him back to bed and hold him to my chest. He presses his face against me, places his hands on my breast, and nurses. "Sylvan," I whisper. My milk flows into him. His hair is downy on his perfectly round head; it smells sweet as honeysuckle. His eyelids flutter and then he opens his eyes and looks up at me.

My child, the one in my belly now. His eyes are blue. Like the antlered king's. His father.

This is what is to be. I only pray that Hex is there, perhaps in the next room, outside the range of my vision. And that wherever I must journey, he will join my child and me. He will forgive me and he will join us.

But that is only the beginning.

As I put my hand to my belly now I think of Storm, Dark, and Swift dying on the Island of Excess Love with feathers molting off their shoulders and the skulls of birds punishing their putrid necks. They killed their king and destroyed the world of illusion. It is too late to redeem them.

Then I think of Acacia, my brother's future wife, sitting on those rocks, shivering, staring out at the empty seas, empty except for us in our little boat. I think of the young men and women, whom Acacia called the brothers and sisters, and their white steeds clambering over the rocks, watching us leave, looking at us as if they were waiting to be rescued. I had believed that all I wanted was to stay hidden in my home, protecting my loved ones, hoarding our precious water and the glorious magic of fruits and vegetables. But after my journey I no longer believe this. I know that when I have returned, reclaimed and restored my home, won back my beloved, and completed what was begun on the Island of Excess Love, I will have to go out into the world, perhaps numerous times, and find the ones who remain. I must help them any way I can.

This is my destiny; now I know. And it has not quite even yet begun.

AUTHOR'S NOTE

While my previous book *Love in the Time of Global Warming* is loosely based on Homer's *Odyssey*, *The Island of Excess Love* is even more loosely inspired by Virgil's *Aeneid*. In that epic a Greek army, hidden in the belly of a wooden horse, attacks the city of Troy. The hero Aeneas escapes with his son, Ascanius, his father Anchises, and some warriors, and then ventures out into the world to create a new home for his people. After much danger, loss, and sacrifice, including a tragic love affair with Queen Dido, and a journey to the underworld, Aeneas finally founds the city of Rome. The story is about, among other things, perseverance in the face of adversity.

Although some of the themes in *The Island of Excess Love* are similar, I have taken many liberties with the story and not all characters in this book correspond directly to characters in *The Aeneid*. As mentioned, it served more as an inspiration than anything else and I am very grateful to have the words of Virgil (translated by the wonderful C. Day Lewis) to guide me. I hope you enjoyed this tale and that you turn to the original text to find out more and to discover inspiration of your own.

Francesca Lia Block
September 27, 2013
Los Angeles, California

Moweaqua Public Library
600 N. Putnam
Moweaqua, IL 62550